Machine Without Horses

Also by Helen Humphreys

Fiction

Leaving Earth

Afterimage

The Lost Garden

Wild Dogs

Coventry

The Reinvention of Love

The Evening Chorus

Non-Fiction

The Frozen Thames

Nocturne

The River

The Ghost Orchard

Machine Without Horses

A NOVEL

Helen Humphreys

HarperCollinsPublishersLtd

Machine Without Horses

Published by HarperCollins Publishers Ltd

First edition

HarperCollins books may be purchased for educational, business, or sales promotional use through our Special Markets Department.

HarperCollins Publishers Ltd
Bay Adelaide Centre, East Tower
22 Adelaide Street West, 41st Floor
Toronto, Ontario, Canada
M5H 4E3

www.harpercollins.ca

Library and Archives Canada Cataloguing in Publication information is available upon request.

ISBN 978-1-44343-249-8

Printed and bound in the United States
LSC/H 9 8 7 6 5 4 3 2 1

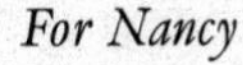

For Nancy

From the bottom of the pool, fixed stars
Govern a life.

—"Words," Sylvia Plath

Machine Without Horses

Part One

She has never seen a fish before. She stands in the shallows of the river, the water tightening its wire of cold around her knees, while her father calls her name from shore. She bends instead to the pattern of ripples on the surface, to the flutter of the salmon below, drifting slowly past her feet like large, dark birds.

I.

WHAT I CAN DO IN DARKNESS: MAKE LOVE, negotiate my way through the dim hallways of my house, talk on the phone, drink a glass of water. What she could do in darkness: tie a fishing fly.

It is the hottest summer I can remember. No rain for six weeks. The fields crisping at their edges, and the trees rattling with dry leaves, slowly dying from the ground up.

Perhaps it is this yearning for water that attracts me to the idea of her, to the real-life Megan Boyd, who tied exquisite salmon flies for sixty-odd years in a small Scottish cottage, without electricity or running water, and who, although she made the world's best flies, never fished herself.

She said she made the lures for the fishermen, not for the fish—meaning that she had no desire to kill the salmon, yet her flies were helping the fishermen do just that. An odd logic, but that is what I find fascinating about her. She was a woman of extremes.

How do you become the best at something that you yourself have never tested? How do you separate an object from its purpose?

I am making notes about Megan Boyd—her life, the flies she made, the little bits of information that exist about her character—trying to tie these fragments into a story. I am sitting on my couch, with the ceiling fan turning its frantic circles above my head and the dog curled up beside me, while outside, the world bakes and shrivels. The brown grass has dried to needles. The roses are blown out against the fence.

I wasn't looking for Megan Boyd as a subject to write about. As with so much of the writing life, she appeared by accident.

The onslaught of heat has made a lot of things impossible and it is difficult to be outside for any length of time. Usually, in summer, I spend all my hours outdoors, loathe to come inside even when it is dark. But now, forced to remain in the house, I have had to change my habits. One of the activities I decided on was to (finally) tidy my study, an upstairs room crammed with books and piles of papers and barely ever entered because it is too much of a mess and feels oppressive the instant I step through the door.

But there, in the first stack of papers I start through, is the *New York Times* obituary for Megan Boyd, given to me years ago by a friend who thought the famous fly dresser would make an interesting story, and filed away for future consideration.

The sun angles in the second-floor window, and the air through the screen is humid and close. I read the obituary. Megan Boyd is described as eccentric and a perfectionist. The fishing fly named after her is for use in the dead of summer, when the heat makes the salmon disinclined to bite.

I close my eyes and imagine standing in the cool shallows of a river. I cast my mind upstream, to the rock pools and the hills, to the low-roofed tin shed where Megan Boyd worked with such solitary dedication.

When I open my eyes again, my world has shifted.

The beginning of a life is often the start of the story. Character is formed from early incidents and accidents, from sudden trauma, or reassuring constancy. These are more important than aspects of personality because they are the ground on which the inherent nature of the person blossoms or is stifled.

Rosina Megan Boyd was born on January 29, 1915, in Surrey, England. She was the youngest of three children. In 1918, at the end of the First World War, her father took a job on the Sutherland estate near Brora, Scotland. The family moved with him, and Megan's early life, and first real memories, took place in the remote and starkly beautiful landscape surrounding the River Brora.

In various accounts of Megan Boyd's life, Megan's father has been called a "baliff," a "riverwatcher" and a "gillie," so perhaps his job was a mix of all three. A baliff and riverwatcher are similar, in that the person undertaking these jobs has a custodial duty towards the river. He is on the lookout for people who are breaching the fishing regulations—poachers, and those who don't have a valid licence or who are fishing out of season or exceeding the catch limits. A gillie is more of a guide to the fishermen. He will know the best places on the river to fish, the pools where the salmon rest during their journey upstream, and he will give advice on which flies to use given the weather and seasonal conditions.

It is a beautiful notion: watching a river for a job, for an entire working life, knowing the habits of the creatures that live in and along the water, determining the effects of weather and season on the workings of the river. It seems to me a perfect job, and while I do a little research on the River Brora, I let myself imagine Megan as a small child, trailing behind her father as he strides along the banks of the river or bends down to peer into a rock pool. He would have talked to her, shown her things, answered her questions. She would have seen the dark shudder of the salmon moving below the surface of the water, the trills of light played out on the ripples above. She would have heard the sound of the moving river, felt its coolness weave through her open fingers. Putting her hand to her mouth, Megan would have tasted the tang of the river on her tongue.

I moved when I was very young, and like Megan's, it was a move from one distinct landscape to another. She moved from Surrey to Scotland. I moved from Surrey to Canada. I don't know what the effect of the move was like for Megan, but for me it manifested in a strong need to attach myself to my new surroundings.

Megan attached to the River Brora so completely that she knew it as intimately as her father did and would advise the fishermen who came to buy her flies that they would need one fly if it was sunny out, a different one if it was cloudy, another for the rain, so subtle and definitive were the weather changes on the mood of the salmon.

The River Brora begins in the Ben Armine mountains in the north of Scotland and runs 165 miles to empty into the North Sea. It moves through Loch Brora, and the last three miles of the river are fast, with rapids and pools, as it hurries through the end of its journey. There are twenty named pools on the river, including one that is over two hundred yards long. Some of the names of the pools are descriptive or evocative: Flats, Chemist's, Snag, Madman and the Magazine. The salmon begin moving into the mouth of the river in late January and continue until the end of the season in mid-October, so, with various surges in the spring and early fall, there are almost continuous salmon on the River Brora.

The dog is restless, so I take her out. It's too hot to walk across the brown, crunchy grass, and even too hot for the woods, so I take her down to a river near Kingston to swim. Charlotte has never been one to chase a stick, but she will splash around in the shallows, biting at the water for a while, and then, when she is good and wet, we can stroll slowly through the small patch of woods back to the car and both feel satisfied that we have had an outing.

It's just the dog and me these days. Which is okay, for now. I've had five deaths in six years and the sudden gust of that has made me feel wobbly, off balance, not able to do much more than take the simplest path through my days. Animals are good for sorrow because they don't make a fuss about anything and have fairly uncomplicated expectations for the day-to-day.

Maybe I like the idea of Megan Boyd because I can picture her colourful, beautiful lures arcing out of the darkness towards me in a simple, perfect line. And like the salmon, I want to leap towards the fly, marry it, swallow it, because its brightness feels like an answer to sadness.

Megan's father presented her with her first salmon fly when she was a child. She thought it was "pretty." That was her word for it. The fly was a Blue Charm, a popular low-water summer fly from the early years of the twentieth century. The blue, from a tiny piece of cockerel feather, was apparently attractive to the salmon in the blue light of early morning.

Starting a book is like starting a love affair. It demands full and tireless attention or feelings could change. Commitment takes time, and so there must be a rush of passion at the beginning. This means that the other life of the writer, the "real life," has to fade into the background for a while. In the past I have found this difficult, but now it is a relief. At the moment, real life is overrated and I am happy to think about the River Brora and to imagine Megan's childhood near it.

2.

MEGAN LEARNED TO TIE FLIES AT THE AGE of twelve from Bob Trussler, a gillie who worked with her father on the Sutherland estate. Trussler took apart salmon flies and then made Megan reassemble them, using smaller and smaller hooks. She must have shown promise at the task and received praise from both men, for she seemed to have made the decision that fly-tying would be her vocation from this early game. She left school at fourteen and left home at twenty. Her first job, furnished through her father, was to repair or re-tie all the salmon flies in a fisherman's tackle box, for which she was paid five pounds. With this money, she bought her father a new three-piece wool suit from the Army and Navy Stores in London and still had enough cash left over to purchase the materials she needed to set herself up in business.

She lived in a small cottage on the Kintradwell estate, a few miles up the road from Brora. The cottage had no electricity or running water. Megan tied her flies in a shed on the property, using a kidney-shaped dressing table as her work surface. Aside from the lessons from Bob Trussler, she depended on advice from the classic volume *How to Dress Salmon Flies: A Handbook for Amateurs* by T.E. Pryce-Tannatt and published in 1914. She called this book her "bible."

Initially, Megan's father and Trussler supplied her with clients for her salmon flies, from the collection of fishermen who hired them as guides on the River Brora. But soon, she was attracting clients from elsewhere as her reputation for tying perfect salmon flies grew and spread. In the middle of her life, at the height of her fame, Megan Boyd had orders from all over the world and was operating on a four-year backlog.

Why do we do the things we do? Why do we have the jobs we have? Choice or lack of choice. Circumstance and opportunity. Realizing that you are good at something is a strong motivation to continue. It is hard not to take praise to heart and be encouraged by it. Perhaps pleasing her father and Bob Trussler by tying "pretty" salmon flies was enough for Megan. She never felt the need to look elsewhere for her purpose in life. She had approval for what she did, and a built-in client base. It seems like a practical choice. And yet it was also bound up in sentiment—her relationship with her father, who others said was miserable and cantankerous, her attraction to the "pretty" pattern of the Blue Charm, its delicate, intricate balance of feather and thread.

Making a salmon fly is about doing it right. It is about constructing something absolutely perfectly and then being able to replicate that act over and over again. It is also about knowing the fish and what they will and won't like. The salmon who run the rivers aren't there to feed. They have done their feeding for years in the North Atlantic, gorging on sand eels, krill and herring. Now they are on their way back up the rivers they were born in, to spawn. So, they are not responding to a fishing fly out of appetite. They do not need to take it, thinking it is an insect. They are not operating from hunger, which is probably the level we are all operating from most of the time—physical hunger for sustenance, but also emotional hunger, sexual desire, and even spiritual hunger. So, what does it mean to choose to take something that you don't want or need?

Megan had a theory that the salmon retained memories of the young aquatic insects they had eaten in the rivers when they were young parr, and that they would take a salmon fly because it triggered this memory. They had returned to the rivers they were born in by remembering the particular scent of their native river, and in entering that river they were entering their own pasts, so it makes sense that they would respond to something that reminded them of that past.

So highly did Megan regard the judgment and instincts of the salmon that she would never cut a feather or bit of fur, because a cut mark is not natural and the fish would recognize that and leave the fly alone.

When I set about making a story, one of the first things I think about is the motivation of the main character. What is it that they want? What are they driven by? Story is created from combining a character's motivation with their circumstances. For example, if a character wants to be rich and they are born into abject poverty, then the story is about their struggle to achieve what they desire, with their motivation set against their circumstances. If they succeed, the story is a triumph. If they fail, it is a tragedy. The more extreme the distance between the motivation of the character and the situation they find themselves in, the more epic the sweep of the story.

What did Megan Boyd want? What did tying salmon flies give her that she couldn't get elsewhere?

It's a question I can't easily answer, so I make a move sideways. I have decided that I should take some fly-tying lessons myself, in order to better understand what Megan Boyd did, and so I spend the rest of the morning following leads until I have found someone to teach me. I make an appointment for the next day and then take the dog out through the woods. It is still stiflingly hot, but it feels good to be away from the house.

The ground is cracked along the forest path, deep fissures splitting the earth. I drop a small pebble down one of them and it disappears. No sound of it hitting the bottom of the rut.

At the river, I look for salmon, even though I know it is too early in the season. The salmon still run this city river, in spring and fall, arching their bodies against the current upriver, on their way to spawn. I like to watch them muscling through the water, negotiating the rocks and each other, and the fishers who stand in the river, arcing their lines upstream.

Dog walkers are routine creatures, and I often recognize them by their dogs and the time of day they are out. At a bend in the river, I meet the French bulldog, George, and the man who owns him. I usually see them at least once a week. We stand politely for a moment, exchanging pleasantries as our dogs sniff each other, and then we all break apart and continue our walks. It is not unusual, as a dog owner, to know George's name and not know the name of the man who accompanies him.

At night, I lie in bed and think of what Megan could want, what her motivations were. Praise? Is this enough to fuel a whole lifetime? I'm not sure. The work of tying flies would be monotonous, full of repetition, hard on the eyes and hands. I imagine her hunched over her makeshift workbench with the sun slanting in the window—for she only worked in natural light, starting when the sun rose in the morning and ending her day when it set at night. She has the fishing hook fixed in the vise and is winding the first layer of black thread onto the shank. Next, she will add a tiny bit of feather or a thin strip of silver tinsel. Perhaps she is listening to the radio while she works. (There is a radio on the shelf behind her desk in one of the photos I have of her fly-tying shed.) Maybe her dog is there, keeping her company. In another photo I have seen of her workspace, her border collie, Patch, sits right beside her, watching carefully as she ties a lure, looking more like a reproachful assistant than a pet.

There is a rhythm to the work, a familiar rhythm, and she can enter it the way one enters a river, letting it wash over her. The angle of sunlight. The winding of the thread over the hook. Voices on the radio. The presence of the dog. Company and solitude. The habit of familiar work in the changing light of a new day. What did she make of it all? What were her thoughts?

I turn over and watch the street light out the window, the way it haloes the little piece of pavement at its base. Megan Boyd would have turned in bed and seen only blackness out of her window—a spill of stars on a clear night, and the soft hush of the sea beyond her garden.

3.

My brother.

My father.

Three close friends.

(Not in that order.)

(My dog, who, I know, is not the same as a person, but thirteen years . . .)

4.

THE SALMON FLY–TYING TEACHER'S NAME IS Paul. He lives an hour away, in a neat bungalow on the weedy end of a small lake. He comes out to meet my car as I negotiate between the tidy flower beds, full of white gravel and wilted geraniums.

"Welcome!" he says, spreading his arms wide in what I first mistake for the expectation of a hug and then realize is just a magnanimous gesture. He is wearing khaki shorts that have creases down the front from being ironed and a clean white quick-dry shirt with the sleeves rolled up. It is nine o'clock in the morning and he is already sweating.

I open the back door of the car and Charlotte bounds out, totally ignoring Paul and hurtling over the parched grass to the lake, where she throws herself off the dock with abandon into the shallow, reedy water. She emerges covered with mud and streaks of algae, shaking herself vigorously at the lake edge, then immediately gets down to the serious business of hunting frogs.

Paul has a dismayed expression on his face, watching Charlotte nosing through the weeds.

"You said I could bring her," I say, which sounds petulant and ruder than I mean it to.

"I know. It's just . . ." Paul trails off, his eyes still on the dog's movements.

"I'm sorry," I say. "I just couldn't leave her alone all day. She'll stay outside. She prefers that."

Paul leads me, reluctantly it seems, into the bungalow. It's noticeably cooler indoors, the whir of the window air conditioner like a jet engine.

The house is decorated like a fussy old person's house, with frills and wallpaper borders and cute sayings on the walls. *Home Is Where the Heart Is. New Friends Are Silver, Old Friends Are Gold.* There are knick-knacks on every surface, but it is not disordered, just cluttered.

I think that Paul might live with his mother, even though he seems to be in his early fifties, like me. There is, however, no sign of another human being in the house.

"I tie my flies in the basement," he says, and

I follow him through a dark panelled hallway to a rickety set of basement stairs at the back of the house.

This is clearly his domain. I can't imagine an old person negotiating the twisted rack of stairs or ducking under the low-hanging beams. He definitely lives with his mother, I think. It is classic child to escape to the basement—sadly, even a child in his fifties.

It is cooler underground. Paul leads me to a long table buttressed up against the far wall.

"I tried to clean up," he says, "but it's a messy hobby." He waves his hand over the feathers and spools of thread, the open boxes of what look like animal pelts.

"Please." He pulls out a chair for me, and when I sit down, he sits down right next to me.

It feels awkwardly like a date for the first few moments, until he hands me a vise, shows me how to clamp it onto the tabletop, next to his vise.

"If we are side by side, then you can see exactly what I'm doing," he says, switching on a standing lamp. "It's the best way to learn."

I think of the photo of Megan Boyd sitting next to her dog at her workbench. I am clearly the dog in this scenario.

"I read about your lady," Paul says. "Seems she was quite the legend in salmon fly circles."

"One of the best," I say.

Paul wipes his palms and forehead with a small orange towel, then folds it carefully and puts it down next to his glasses case on the far right-hand side of the table.

"Well," he says, "unfortunately, I am not one of the best, so I won't be able to help you tie flies like she could. But I think I can break down the process for you, and maybe that will help."

"Anything will help," I confess. "I'm trying to work my way inside her mind before I write about her."

"Very interesting." Paul draws out the word *very.* He passes me a bobbin of black thread. "This is what we use to tie all the materials onto the hook. But first, we lay down a base layer of thread to cover the metal. All we're going to do this morning is work on laying down the thread. Practice will build confidence, and the base layer needs to be applied with confidence, but not so much that you disregard what it is you are doing."

This seems like good advice for almost anything in life, and I am relieved that he is teaching me to tie flies in manageable segments. This is also how I like to write, never looking too far into the distance in case I become overwhelmed by the magnitude of work that lies ahead.

Tying flies is, of course, harder than it looks, and requires keeping a consistent tension on the hand that controls the bobbin, to ensure that the thread wraps around the hook with an even tautness and doesn't overlap.

I wind the thread on the hook, then unwind it, then wind it back on again. Paul checks each time. He is stingy with praise, only saying "better" or "not bad" to signal my progress. After an hour and a half of wrapping and unwrapping the hook, he declares a break, scraping back his chair on the rough cement floor and bouncing to his feet.

"Come upstairs," he says. "I have some iced tea in the fridge."

The dog is still after frogs at the edge of the lake, but when she hears the back door open, she comes bounding up onto the porch, barking sharply to reprimand me for disappearing for so long. I rub her ears and she hangs around for a minute or two, then rushes back to the shoreline.

"I don't really understand dogs," says Paul, watching her. "I've always been a cat person myself."

"Do you have a cat?" Charlotte likes nothing

better than to chase cats. For her, it's right up there with hunting frogs as one of life's ultimate pleasures. The thought of the potential carnage makes me nervous.

"Not anymore," he says. "The last one just disappeared. I think she was eaten by a coyote." He takes a sip of his tea. "Sophie," he says a little sadly. "She was a tortoiseshell. Very pretty."

The word *pretty* reminds me of Megan Boyd.

"Why do you make flies?" I ask. "Do you fish?"

"Not really. Not anymore." Paul stirs the ice in his drink. "I like the puzzle of it. Making the different lures, following a pattern. Sometimes I sell them or give them away to friends or neighbours. I've always been good with my hands, I guess. I used to make model airplanes when I was young. Complicated ones. I made an aircraft carrier once, with a whole deck load of tiny individual fighter jets." He takes another sip of iced tea. "Can I ask you a question?" he says.

"Sure."

"How do you get inside someone's head to write about them? Especially someone who was a real person?"

This is the sixty-million-dollar question, and one that I don't really have a definitive answer for because I'm constantly shifting my thinking about how to accomplish this kind of transference. It is hard enough to be oneself. How can we effectively become someone else?

"I suppose I try and level the playing field," I say. "Occupy as much of their experience as I can. Learning to tie salmon flies, for example. Finding commonalities."

"But their thoughts?"

"That's trickier. I have to take a guess at it. But hopefully, by the time I get there, it's an educated guess and will seem believable because I've done the work of learning who Megan Boyd was."

"Yes." Paul nods his head in agreement. "That makes sense."

We go back to the basement and I wind thread for another hour, and then Paul sends me on my way. I am to return every morning for a week, at the end of which time, he promises, I will know how to make a Jock Scott, which is one of the salmon flies that Megan used to tie.

The dog sleeps happily in the air conditioning all the way back to town, her long legs hanging limply over the back seat, her head propped up on the armrest. She never actually catches frogs when she hunts them, isn't much interested in eating them. She just likes how they move. That's what attracts her to them. Similar, perhaps, to how a salmon responds to a fly: it likes how the fly moves through or on top of the water. The fisher *presents* the fly—that is the terminology—as though the fisher is somehow auditioning for the salmon.

That evening, while I'm eating dinner, Paul calls me. He is hesitant on the phone, and it feels strange for him to call me when I will be seeing him the next morning.

"I've been giving it some thought," he says, "and I think you need to look into Megan Boyd's view."

"Her view?"

"What she would have seen out her window when she was tying flies. It matters."

"But you don't see anything when you tie flies?" I say, thinking of the blank cinder-block wall that faced us when we were sitting in Paul's basement this morning.

"It matters," he says again, and then he hangs up.

5.

Cancer.
Cancer.
Cancer.
Cancer.
Cancer.
Cancer. (Even the dog.)

6.

THE SETTING FOR A STORY IS ALMOST AS important as character—in fact, in certain instances, it can operate as a sort of character. So, in thinking about Megan Boyd's immediate landscape, I have to consider how vital a role it played in her life.

Megan's cottage in Kintradwell looked out on the North Sea. That was the view she would see when she looked up from her work and out the window in front of where her desk was positioned. But in the foreground, directly outside, was her garden. Friends remembered the garden as being full of flowers, so she must have spent some time tending it. Past the garden was a fence, then the road, then a strip of rail track, followed by a grassy verge, and beyond the verge was the sand and the sea. Look up and see the water, but look down and see the garden, the road, the train tracks. Six times a day, the train would shunt along the rails—half of those journeys going north and half heading back towards Inverness. The road would have had traffic on it fairly constantly, and if Megan had the windows open, she would have been able to hear the cars, the train and, beyond that, the crash of waves onto the shore if the surf was high. That was a lot of activity to layer onto her solitary pursuit of fly-tying, and I wonder if she was so used to all the noise and movement that she effectively blocked it out, or if it interrupted her work. Did she raise her head every time the train went past? Did she listen for the changes in the sound of the sea as it hurled itself against the shingle? How much attention did she pay to the outside world when she was engrossed in tying her salmon flies? Did the constant movement beyond her cottage window make her restless, or did the outside activity make her cleave more solidly to her solitude and stillness?

The main question to ask about setting in a novel is to determine what is private and what is public. What does everyone know about the place where the story is set, and what will only the main character know?

During the Second World War, when Megan Boyd was in her twenties, she helped the war effort by delivering milk and working as a coastwatcher or warden for the little stretch of coastline near her house. One of those activities is inherently social and one is inherently solitary, and I wonder if, in combination, they set the tone for her life to follow. Because although Megan lived in isolation, she was not isolated. She had a lot of visitors to her cottage—fishermen there to buy her flies or to regale her with stories of the catches they had made with those flies. She was also involved in village life, participating in Scottish country dances and helping the young and the elderly. So, she would have had intimate knowledge of where she lived and of the people who lived near her.

A fisherman said that Megan was so used to tying flies that she could do it without looking. That meant she would have often been looking out the window, instead of down at the lure. Those years of volunteering as a coastwatcher, of staring out to sea in search of enemy aircraft or submarines, might have become a habit. But after the war, when she wasn't looking for trespassing planes on the patch of North Sea beyond her window, what was she looking at? Was the shifting pattern of the water and light enough to keep her attention for decades? Or was it more of a Zen approach, where staring at the sea was a form of meditation while she was working on tying salmon flies?

I have a lot more questions about Megan's landscape than I can answer, and I wonder, briefly, whether it would be a good idea to go to Brora and look around for myself. But I'm not sure that would do any good because I would be looking at everything with fresh eyes, and so I would only see the "public" face of the area and would not be able to experience Megan's private view of her surroundings. Also, she has been dead for fifteen years at this point, so things will have changed with her cottage and environs. So, that will be the part of the story that I will have to largely invent, a thought that feels uncomfortable because there are multitudes of ways to get it wrong.

The trouble with writing a novel is that there are so many ways to make mistakes that you just have to give up on the idea of getting it right. Instead, you have to choose a few aspects to remain faithful to and do your best to make everything else as believable as possible for the reader. In this story, I will try to capture Megan's character and hope for the best as far as the landscape goes. Research and some knowledge of Scotland will hopefully be enough to adequately replicate the landscape around Brora in words.

Although a small town, Brora has an industrial past. Coal was consistently mined there since the sixteenth century, and it was the site of the most northerly coal mine in the British Isles. That mine closed for good in 1974, after over four hundred years of production.

The tiny Brora harbour was home to a herring fishing fleet in the nineteenth century, and there was also textile manufacturing in town, brick and tile plants, and salt production. The harbour was also the location of a boat-building operation. A whisky distillery was introduced to the area in the nineteenth century and still operates there today, and a woollen mill was opened in the early twentieth century, selling upmarket tweed clothing.

The railway came to Brora in 1871 and the radio in 1939, two important connections to the outside world. In its nineteenth-century heyday, when all enterprises were in gainful operation, the population of the town was close to two thousand people. Now it hovers around twelve hundred. In Megan's day, it would have had a few hundred more people than it does now.

The buildings of Brora, like the buildings of Kingston, where I live, are made of limestone, and there were several limestone quarries in proximity to the town in the nineteenth century. Inhabitants of the town described the dull grey buildings as being depressing in the winter, which is a sentiment uttered in my town as well. But I like to think that the opposite is true. Limestone is made from compressed sea creatures from prehistoric, living seas. The building blocks of both Brora and Kingston are a congress of dead sea creatures from the ancient slip and spill. Each stone older than all of human life.

7.

I FIRST WENT TO SCOTLAND WHEN I WAS IN my early twenties, with my boyfriend at the time. It was early summer and the sky was light late into the evening. We began our journey in Edinburgh and then took the train north to Perth. After that, we hitch-hiked farther east, ending up on our first night in the small coastal village of Crail on the edge of the North Sea. It was a beautiful spot and the day was sunny and flawless. We walked the narrow streets for a while upon arrival, and then went to a pub for supper before heading back to our bed and breakfast for the night.

My boyfriend was someone I had known a long time. We grew up near to each other and were good friends when we were children. I fully expected that I would marry him, and on that trip, on that night in Crail, he asked me to, as we were walking along the harbour wall after our meal. He said, "But sleep on it," and I agreed.

The next morning, I woke before him, just as it was getting light out. I dressed quickly and left the room, walking back down to the harbour.

It was low tide and there were suddenly all these rock pools along the shore that hadn't been there the previous day, when the tide had extended right up to the harbour wall. I wandered among the pools, looking at the seaweed and stranded sea creatures. A little way ahead of me, on the foreshore, were two women, slightly older than me, doing exactly what I was doing. They were giddy with laughter, clutching on to each other as they clambered over the slippery rocks, bending down together to peer at a crayfish or a shell. We were the only people out this early. Above us, the village and, presumably, my boyfriend were still asleep.

I followed the women. I couldn't help myself. Not wanting to disturb them, I kept a respectful distance, but I stopped watching the tidal pools at my feet and turned my attention on them. What I liked was their laughter and ease with each other, their intimacy. It took me a while to realize that they were a couple, not simply friends, and when

I did realize that, I also realized something else. It shocked me to recognize that I wasn't as happy as they were, and I knew I wanted to be that happy.

I went back to the bed and breakfast and told my boyfriend that I couldn't marry him.

8.

There's a cow that has escaped from a farm that borders the woods in Kingston where I take the dog to walk. She's been missing for three weeks now, turning up now and then to be photographed with someone's phone, but when the farmer goes looking for her, she has disappeared again. She's large and brown and the one news report I heard about her said that she "should not be approached." She doesn't look very scary in the blurry phone photograph that's online, and I like thinking of her on the lam, maybe joining up with the wild deer that occasionally roam this piece of land.

I meet George and his human near the entrance to the wood.

"Did you hear about the cow?" I ask, while our dogs stiffly renew their acquaintance.

"I have been looking for it," he confesses. "I mean, how can a cow stay hidden for so long? It's a big animal and a small wood."

The presence of something unusual in our usual routines is always startling and exciting. I once saw a buck cross the grass by the river and thought about it for weeks afterwards, the sighting feeling like a sort of magic that I appliqued to everything in my ordinary world.

I took the dog for a walk before heading up to Paul's, hoping to burn off some of her frog-hunting energy, but the moment we turn into his driveway, even after an hour in the woods, she is churning around the back seat, waiting for the glorious moment of release when I open the door and she can fly downhill to the lake.

"She doesn't waste any time, does she?" says Paul, as we watch her mad, unstoppable flight into the water.

"Waiting's not really her strong suit," I say, following him into the house.

He's wearing a different pair of clean, ironed shorts this morning, another immaculate collared shirt, this one a pale yellow. I have on the clothes I wore yesterday. No change at all. Another condition of novel-writing, trying to exist in the world of the book and not the "real" world, so minimizing the choices of that world. When I'm working on a book, I just wear the same clothes day after day, eat the same food with no variation. Novel-writing and depression have a great deal in common, as it turns out.

"I thought about what you said," I say, as we descend the basement stairs. "On the phone. About Megan Boyd's view. I think she was probably looking out to sea most hours of the day for about sixty years."

"She was connected to the salmon then, even without thinking about them." Paul pulls the chair out for me, an unexpected gesture of chivalry that makes me feel awkward.

"Yes, I guess so."

"The salmon were swimming around, feeding, and she was tying the flies that would catch them in a year or two." Paul sits down as well. "It's like time travel."

I hadn't thought of it in those terms before, but I like the association. I like to think of Megan tying flies in her cottage while the fish that will die by those flies swim freely in the ocean, months and years away from being killed, with no knowledge of that fact.

"You're a bit of a philosopher," I say, and Paul grins, pleased with the comment.

"Don't think that flattery will make this next part of the Jock Scott any easier," he says.

I wind a layer of black thread onto my hook, pleased that it goes smoothly today after all the time spent practising it yesterday. Overtop of that, Paul has me wind on some silver tinsel, and overtop of that, a layer of yellow floss. Now I am ready for the first tie-in, which is a small section of golden pheasant feather.

"Always hard to get one that isn't twisted," says Paul, passing me a small section of feather. "This one isn't too bad."

The little piece of pheasant feather is known as the "tail" of the fly. Paul shows me how to strip back a few of the barbs from the base end of the feather, to reveal a smooth section that I can then attach near the hook.

"Don't touch the feather too much or you'll wreck it," says Paul, watching me try to fluff up the top end of it. "The less you handle the components of the fly, the better."

There are many bits and pieces to the Jock Scott. It is a complicated fly pattern, and probably I should have started with something much easier, but I liked the idea of tying a fly that Megan regularly tied, and Paul had suggested the Jock Scott because it is a fly he works on regularly himself.

It is delicate work to tie a fishing fly, and there are many people who assumed that Megan Boyd was so good at it because she was a woman and her hands were small and adept. But from the photos I have seen of her at work in her fly-tying shed, her fingers were thick as sausages, and her hands looked like a mechanic's hands, heavy and muscular. They actually looked bigger than most men's hands.

Paul's hands are small, his fingers thin, his nails clean and scrubbed. I like how he pours all of his attention into the tips of his fingers, the care that he takes in winding on the thread to secure his scrap of pheasant feather. He performs the task with both patience and confidence, and I think of how repetition breeds confidence, of how my years of writing have given me a confidence I never had before.

I have been writing for so long now that I can no longer separate myself from the act of writing. I don't know where one begins and another ends. There was a time when it bothered me that I had become what I did, that I tended to look at everything in terms of story or image, that while I was experiencing my life, I was also apart from it. But I have made peace with that now because what I know about writing is that it will take everything I can throw at it, and that is a comfort. I can fall into it and it will absorb my sorrow, my ideas, my restlessness. It has become a process for making me whole again whenever the world breaks me down.

I think it must have been the same for Megan Boyd. She was good at tying flies because she had a knack for it, and because she did it ceaselessly, and the constant work of it and the praise she received for the finished product would have given her confidence. She could tie flies without looking at them. That implies a level of familiarity and knowledge that is enviable, and it would be accompanied by the self-possession that comes from immersing oneself wholly in one's work.

9.

The real Jock Scott was a gillie who worked for a lord with the same family name: Lord John Scott. The former invented the fly for the latter in 1845. It is one of the most complicated fishing fly patterns, with over fifty different components.

Jock Scott, the gillie, began tying flies around the same age as Megan Boyd, and he first entered the employ of Lord Scott when he was thirteen. The story goes that Lord John Scott met the boy when he was out walking and asked him his name. When he found out that the boy had the same name as he did, he felt it was fortuitous and asked the young Jock Scott to come and work for him. They remained together for twenty-seven years, during which time they formed a strong friendship. Jock Scott was not only a gillie for Lord Scott but also his valet and boxing sparring partner. Their relationship ended when Lord Scott died, at the age of fifty-one, worn out from all his various sporting pursuits, and Jock Scott went on to tie flies for the Earl of Haddington until he died himself, at the age of seventy-six.

Apparently, the original fly was tied using a lock of Lord Scott's wife's red hair for part of the body of the fly. She had what has been described as "titian-coloured" hair. Human hair was sometimes used in salmon flies, as was horse hair. Megan Boyd herself once stopped a small child in Brora who had striking red hair and asked if she could have a swatch of it to use for her flies.

10.

WHO DO WE CONFIDE IN? WHO DO WE TELL our secrets to? It matters that we have someone we can talk to, really talk to. Part of the trouble, for me, of having so many people die at once is that most of my confidants have been wiped out, those intimates I could call up in the middle of the night and who would know what I meant if I spoke about how I was feeling.

Whom did Megan Boyd confide in? Did she ever have a lover?

She worked solidly for six days of the week, from first light to last light, but on Sunday, she took the day off. Friends say she "disappeared" on Sundays, went off in her car in the morning and returned again in the evening. Often, she went to the beautiful "Glen of the Fairies" in Perthshire. It's no surprise that she wanted to make herself scarce, to avoid fishermen dropping by her cottage and asking for flies. (Although, to deal with this eventuality, she left a notebook and pen on a bench outside her door so that people could write down their orders, and she would see to them on her return.) The question is, did she go to meet someone at Glen of the Fairies, or did she spend those Sundays alone?

Glen of the Fairies is a three-hour drive from Brora, a considerable distance for a day trip when there are many other beautiful places to visit that are much closer. So, perhaps the location held a sentimental significance for Megan?

If she were meeting a male lover, it makes sense that he would be a gillie or fisherman, two professions with which she was very familiar. She might have originally met this man because of her fly-tying. He might be a customer, or a friend of a customer. Perhaps he had suggested meeting at Glen of the Fairies because he lived near to there and wanted to show the place to Megan.

I can imagine Megan driving up in her Austin 7 to find her lover waiting for her in the parking lot. What then? A brief embrace? A quick kiss? Then they would walk for a while in the hills, talk over their respective weeks. If her lover was a fisherman,

Megan might give him the flies she had made for him, each one lovingly prepared and handed over proudly. He would praise her work.

"Megan, you spoil me." And she would flush, because it wasn't exactly true, but she liked to hear him say it anyway.

They would spread a blanket on the ground near a beck and have a picnic. It's hard to imagine that Megan was good at either cooking or food preparation, given her spartan living conditions, so I will have to give these tasks to her lover. Let's call him Graham. Perhaps cooking was a hobby for Graham? Or perhaps he was married and just brought leftovers from the larder he shared with his family. Or perhaps he picked up the makings of a ploughman's at the shops—cheese and bread and a jar of Branston pickle.

They would eat the food, slowly, and Megan would exclaim over it, even if it was the exact same meal that they had enjoyed together last Sunday. Her dog would have accompanied them and would lie a little apart from the couple, facing into the hills, guarding them from possible danger. They would toss the dog the heel of the bread. They would drink tea from a flask, maybe enjoy a bottle or two of beer with their picnic lunch.

Maybe they made love on that blanket? Certainly they kissed and murmured endearments to each other. It is hard to imagine Megan having sex, but this is because all the photographs of her that I can find have her well into her sixties—matronly and stout, with her hair cut by herself into an Eton crop, wearing a tweed skirt and a man's suit jacket and tie. I have no pictures of her younger self, of the woman she would have been in her twenties and thirties, even forties, which are the ages at which I am imagining she had a lover.

If it were a man she was meeting, and she was only meeting him on Sundays, then my guess would be that he was married. That was the day perhaps that his wife visited her parents, or was busy at church, and he could slip away on the pretext of one chore or another. That was also why Megan made the long drive to Glenshee, because their time was limited and, to make the most of it, she did the bulk of the travelling.

Glenshee, or "Glen of the Fairies," has a romantic history. It takes its name from a Bronze Age standing stone positioned on a hill and said to be the meeting place for the Glenshee "fairies." The road climbing to the summit of Glen Beag had two notorious hairpin turns in Megan's day and was known as the "Devil's

Elbow." The road was once so steep that buses would off-load their passengers at the bottom and make them walk to the top of the 2,200-foot summit. It would be a very dramatic place to have a rendezvous.

Did Graham love Megan?

Yes. Definitely, yes. Aside from the physical attraction, she would have understood him, understood what was important to him. If Graham was a gillie, then Megan would have a real, working knowledge of what he did for a living, and would enjoy listening to his tales of the river he was protecting. If he were a fisherman, she would have advice for him on how to catch salmon, even if she would decline to watch him fish because if he did catch a salmon, it would upset her.

If he was married, then he was taking a risk in having an affair with Megan, so he had to feel the risk was worth it. Only love would have felt equal to the guilt and dangers of infidelity.

What attracts people to each other? An open smile. Strong, capable hands. Pretty-coloured eyes. The easy manner with which someone laughs or talks. Kindness. Confidence. A shared understanding of the world, the weather, the crucial aspects of a life. This thing we call "chemistry," where there is an inexplicable pull between two people, a mix of temperaments and desires that makes something potent of their combined natures.

The Sunday affair could have gone on and on, running at first on the fumes of desire, and later on friendship and mutual compassion. Nothing need bring it to its close, save for the death of one of the principals, or if the married lover moved away from the area, or if his wife discovered the liaison and put an end to it. At which point, Megan might still have journeyed to Glen of the Fairies on Sundays, but now to visit the spots where she had once met Graham, and to remember what they had enjoyed together in the height and heat of their affair.

How does all this change if Megan's lover was a woman instead of a man?

Some things would change, and some would remain exactly the same.

One of the striking facts about Megan Boyd was that she wore men's clothing—always a tie, often a jacket, men's shirts and cardigans with her tweed skirts. In the country dances, she always danced the male roles. So, was this a question of gender identity or sexual preference, or was it simply because she was her father's daughter and emulated him, carried on being a man, as it were, after he died? Or were men's clothes simply more comfortable for her to wear while she was working at tying flies? Her friends, acquaintances and the people of Brora simply said that she was "eccentric," that she "was just Megan." But Brora was a very small place, and these were the days before queerness had any kind of mainstream presence, was anything other than hidden, ignored and reviled, so "eccentric" might have been the closest word for what today we might think of as lesbian or trans.

What do you call something when there is no language for it at the time? And are you justified in applying labels retrospectively?

Suppose Megan's lover was a woman. Where would she have met her? Perhaps at one of the ceilidhs that Megan attended in the Brora area, or at a dance competition in Inverness. The woman could also have been a fisher, though, for women as well as men fished in the northern Scottish rivers for salmon. (In fact, the record for the largest salmon ever caught in Scotland is held by a woman. In 1922, Georgina Ballantine, the daughter of a gillie, caught a fifty-four-inch salmon on the River Tay in Perthshire with a rod and reel. The monster salmon weighed sixty-four pounds.)

Most certainly Megan's female lover would have been married.

Megan was an anomaly. Another single woman in the same locale was possible, perhaps one still living with her parents and therefore much younger than Megan. Or there could have been a closeted lesbian who was single and was employed as a schoolteacher or textile worker in town. But the likelihood seems slim that they would have first found each other, and then liked each other. More probable is that the woman was married and met Megan at one of the country dances, which she was in the habit of attending alone as her husband had no interest in dancing. This woman would have come to a country dance and danced with Megan, who always took the male role. Maybe they would have flirted, although neither one might have been entirely conscious that that is what they were doing. Certainly, there was an attraction and a little bit of banter. Then the woman would have visited Megan in her cottage, on the pretense of ordering some flies for her husband, who was an avid fisherman, or for herself, if she also fished. The visit couldn't have been during Megan's working hours, for she would have found it hard to take a break, have her mind move away from the stack of orders that waited for her on the workbench. So, it was in the evening, and the woman—let's call her Evelyn—had come after supper, as Megan suggested.

Megan made them tea and they took it out into the garden, for it was summer and the light was performing a long fade across the lawn. If Megan was feeling more bold than nervous, perhaps she poured them each a whisky instead and they went out into the dusk to sit on wooden chairs by the flower beds, the North Sea flat and bright in front of them.

"It's a beautiful spot," said Evelyn. Unbeknownst to her, Megan had tried the chairs out in different locations the previous evening, trying to determine where was the exact perfect place to sit in the garden: the position where the scent from the flowers would mingle with the sparkle of the North Sea to maximum effect.

The women would stay there longer than they should, until the sea darkened and the stars salted the heavens. At first, the talk was general—the village, the countryside—then they would ask each other questions, not too personal, but Evelyn would inquire about Megan's business, about the process of tying flies, and Megan would ask after Evelyn's children. Maybe they would have a second whisky. Maybe they would talk of their childhoods. Perhaps, in the intimacy that darkness enables, one of them would confess her loneliness. It is a troubling thing to admit to loneliness, because by admitting it, the loneliness increases tenfold. So, when Megan walked Evelyn back to her car at the end of the evening, she would only feel this loneliness, and when Evelyn drove shakily down the farm lane, Megan would watch her tail lights until they were out of sight, and when she went back inside her cottage, it wouldn't look cozy anymore, but empty and a little squalid.

There would have to be many evenings such as this before anything could happen physically between Evelyn and Megan. In fact, it is hard to imagine how they would ever cross that line and believe that their association was anything other than a close friendship. They each might have lived their entire lives in Brora without seeing or hearing or knowing of lesbian couples. It wasn't that long ago that male homosexuality was a prosecutable offence, or that the fact of homosexuality within a family or community was considered deeply shameful to all concerned. So, even if Megan and Evelyn had sexual desire for each other, I'm not sure that they would either recognize it or be able to act upon it. To act would be a bold, and perhaps foolhardy, move that both of them might have been too afraid to risk.

So, there would have been endless nights in Megan's garden. The flowers would have grown straggly. The bottle of whisky would have been drunk and another one opened. The frustration and loneliness would have increased beyond bearing, and nothing would now be able to happen between them because they had waited too long.

If their desire was to be acted upon, it couldn't be there, in Megan's garden, a place they had both grown too familiar with over the preceding weeks. It would have to be somewhere else, a singular event perhaps, like a village ceilidh.

So, this is how I imagine it goes.

Megan arrives on time for the ceilidh. Evelyn arrives late. She had argued with her husband before the dance. He had wanted her not to go out that evening.

"You're never at home anymore," he said. And she had relented somewhat, because she did feel guilty about all her absences. She did feel guilty about seeing so much of Megan Boyd and neglecting her family.

Evelyn relented and agreed to stay home that night and forgo the dance, knowing how much she would be missed. Her feelings of guilt prevailed and she decided she needed to put her family first, needed to prove where her loyalties really lay.

The trouble was that her husband had just

wanted to make a point, and after an hour of numbing small talk with his wife, he wandered off to listen to the football match in the lounge, and Evelyn was left drinking cups of cold tea in the kitchen and feeling like she'd made a dreadful miscalculation.

At the dance, Megan goes through the motions, but she can't concentrate properly on the festivities. She is constantly watching the door to the village hall, her breath in her throat every time it opens, and then the corresponding disappointment when the new arrival isn't Evelyn.

She leaves at the break, gulping in the cold night air to stop from crying as she rushes out to her car. And there, running down the lane, her coat unbuttoned and her hair down, is Evelyn.

This is the unguarded moment. This is the beginning they have been waiting for, the one they couldn't make happen for themselves.

To the outsider, it is nothing. One woman expected another to show at a local dance and is disappointed that she doesn't. But to Megan, it is weeks and weeks of emotions so freighted that she is collapsing under the weight of them. And to Evelyn, it is the terrifying realization that it isn't her husband she longs to be with, and though she tries to bury her feelings under duty, she just can't seem to manage this charade tonight. So, they rush at each other, in the darkness of the country lane, with no one else around and the cheerful noise of the music behind them in the overlit hall. I don't think they say a word. They rush at each other and hold on. And then they kiss, and it all begins.

But now what?

For a moment, perhaps this moment in the rutted country lane, with the hall glowing behind them like a lantern, and the soft pass of an owl in the darkness overhead, all will be well. The release of weeks of pent-up emotion will be such a relief, and the expression of shared desire will feel like a miracle to both of them.

It will be a miracle.

They will let it lead them and they will stumble after it, giggling and clumsy, then surprised by the startling clarity of sex, when they get there. They won't waste any more time in Megan's garden. Now they will be in a hurry to get to bed, and Evelyn will stride from her car through the garden, barely noticing the flowers or the long blue line of the sea.

And just when it has them, when they are helpless in the clutches of love and desire, all the other feelings will suddenly return. Evelyn will be awash in the terrible guilt that comes from cheating on her husband and neglecting her family. Megan will feel the shame of what they are doing, will fear being caught out. How can they have a future? If Evelyn leaves her family, she can't just move in with Megan. It's too small a community. They will be ostracized and talked about. A woman is never forgiven for leaving her children. Megan's business will suffer as a consequence. If they move to another community, it will take a while to set up in business again, and she might not be as successful there. They will have no means of support; no one who will accept them or forgive them for what they have done.

Love makes starting over seem possible, but starting over is always harder than it seems, and it becomes less and less appealing, the more time goes by. The sheer willpower it takes to upset a life is considerable, and while it seems, in its initial stages, that love is all sustaining, it isn't, and after the changes have been made, this becomes quickly apparent.

So it ends. Not from lack of feeling, but from lack of opportunity. No one finds out about the affair, partially because no one can even imagine that such a thing could exist. Evelyn stops going to the country dances, spends her evenings at home, trying to coax pleasure out of being with her family. She avoids driving the road past Megan's cottage. She tries not to think of the kisses, the laughter, the way her body felt under Megan's, and eventually, she is mostly successful. Megan just works harder, takes in more orders, disobeys her own rules of only tying flies during daylight hours and starts to ruin her eyes with the smoky light from the paraffin lanterns at night.

But what of Glen of the Fairies? In this attempt at giving Megan Boyd a love life, I have forgotten the one real piece of evidence that might exist for such a fancy.

I think that, in this scenario, Glen of the Fairies was where Evelyn and Megan had gone once, on a perfect, and rare, day out, and all of Megan's subsequent Sunday trips to Glenshee were about remembering what had been, were a sort of memorial to that love.

There are, of course, other things to consider. A friend of mine, who is a doctor, likes to say, "Mostly it's not cancer. Mostly it's just heartburn, or a virus."

Because the simplest explanation is often the correct one.

Once, I had dinner with a famous novelist. He was wearing two different watches, one on each wrist. I asked him why he had on two watches and he said, "I'm going to tell you two different stories, and you tell me which one is the right one."

He pointed to the watch on his left wrist. "This was my father's watch. My parents divorced when I was twelve and I didn't see my father for much of my teenage years. He showed up unexpectedly on my twenty-first birthday and gave me this watch, which he had been given when he was twenty-one by his father. At first, I was angry with him for his long absence and I refused to wear the watch. But later, I came to appreciate the gesture, especially since he died shortly after that exchange. I put the watch on and have never taken it off."

The novelist tapped the face of the watch on his right wrist.

"I bought this watch because the other watch stopped working, and then, when I put this watch on, the first watch suddenly started working again."

I guessed correctly.

The simple explanation is that there was no lover. Megan Boyd had been to visit Glenshee with her parents when she was a child and it held sentimental attachment. Or she had gone there alone, as part of her efforts to acquaint herself with the Scottish wilderness. She enjoyed the landscape and she drove there with her dog, on her one day off each week, wandering through the hills and having her tea out as a treat.

Or, there was someone she was once romantically interested in—a man or a woman, it hardly matters which—and she simply never acted or was unable to act on her feelings. She might have met the person during one of the dance competitions at Inverness. Perhaps there was a group outing the next day to Glen of the Fairies and she spent that day in the company of the man or woman whom she had a crush on, not experienced enough in matters of the heart to know that chances are good that someone for whom you have feelings is likely to also have feelings for you.

But while this may be the "truth," it can't be the story. A story needs drama, incident. A story needs people in it, not simply a woman walking with her dog over the hills, or tying endless salmon flies in the shed in her garden. A story, this story, needs Megan Boyd to have a lover.

II.

WHEN I TAKE THE DOG DOWN TO THE RIVER tonight there is more activity than usual. People are walking along the banks, peering into the water. There are police officers riding their bikes slowly through the woods, looking right and left into the thicket of trees.

"What's going on?" I ask one of the officers by the river. "Is it the missing cow?"

"Cow?" He looks at me like I'm crazy. "It's a missing person." He reaches into his jacket pocket, hands me a photocopy with a picture on it. In the picture, a smiling, handsome man holds a small dog in his arms. I recognize the dog.

"That's George," I say.

"His name is Carlos," says the policeman, plucking the piece of paper from my hand.

"No, the dog. The dog's name is George. I know them. I just saw them yesterday. What's happened?"

"They were spotted walking here a few hours ago and then the dog was found down by the car park, soaking wet. No sign of Carlos Bastida. It looks like he might have gone into the river. His sister said he doesn't know how to swim."

"But the river isn't over a person's head?" I say. In fact, it is lower than usual this year because of the drought. It is probably only up to my knees in the deepest part. It seems impossible to drown in something that shallow.

The policeman shrugs, bored of my questions. "The dog was wet. The man can't swim. This is what we have to go on. If you see anything on your walk, let us know." He hands me a business card and moves off in one direction, while I move off in the other.

It is unsettling to think of someone disappearing while doing something so banal as walking a dog. Also, it is hard not to think that something awful has happened to Carlos if his dog has shown up without him. I turn away from the river and head back into the shelter of the woods.

12.

Paul is in a strange mood when I arrive at his house the next morning. He isn't waiting in the driveway when I pull in. I have to knock on his front door, and when he appears, his face is red and his hair is askew. He is wearing yet another immaculate shorts and shirt ensemble, but I can't shake the feeling that he has been crying as he leads me, wordlessly, down the hallway of his bungalow, towards the rickety basement stairs.

When we are seated in our side-by-side fly-tying seats, which I have come to think of as being the cockpit of an airplane—pilot and co-pilot—Paul just stares at his vise, his hands immobile in his lap.

"Are you okay?" I ask.

"I should never have let you tie the Jock Scott," he says, without looking at me. "It's too difficult a fly. You will just make a hash of it."

This is rather harsh criticism, considering that I have done a fair job of laying down the base layer of thread and tinsel and tying in the pheasant tail.

"Well, I just need to go through the motions," I say. "For research purposes. I have your example to study for how the fly should actually look."

"I appreciate your helping me," I add.

"All well and good," he says. "But what's the point?"

I have no idea what he's talking about.

"I like that you're a writer," Paul says. "I don't usually have writers as clients. It's mostly fishermen. I thought it would be an interesting change."

"And isn't it?"

"You don't understand."

"Well, explain it then." I am losing patience with his halting way of communicating. He has probably spent more time alone than with people, working first on model airplanes and then on fishing flies. I have a flash of thinking that perhaps Megan Boyd wasn't good at communicating either. Perhaps her exchanges were limited to remarks about her fishing flies or the weather. Perhaps she excelled at country dancing because it was a mute pastime.

Paul pushes back his chair abruptly. "Follow me," he says, and heads back across the basement to the staircase.

In the kitchen, he leads me over to the fridge and wrenches open the freezer door.

"I can't eat them," he says.

I peer into the ice-encrusted box and see a neat stack of trays. Each tray appears to have a piece of masking tape affixed to it, with writing on it. I can only read the top label. It says, "Tuesday."

"Someone made you this food and you don't want to eat it?" I say. "Your mother?" Because, despite any hard evidence, I can't give up on the notion that Paul lives with his mother.

"My wife." He leans his head against the door. Puffs of vapour drift from the freezer, like smoke.

"She left you?"

"She died."

I reach into the compartment, lift up the first tray to read the label on the tray beneath. "Monday." The tray under that one reads, "Sunday."

"Jesus," I say. "She cooked for you and then she died."

"She cooked for me while she was dying," says Paul. "During those really hot July days. Before she went into hospital for the last time."

"She died in July?"

"Just over a month ago."

"Jesus," I say again. This is more recent than

the most recent of my deaths. "I can't believe you're coping at all, let alone teaching some idiot to tie a salmon fly."

Paul smiles at that. "You're not really an idiot," he says.

"All things are relative," I say.

The cool of the freezer air feels good where it wafts against my forehead.

"You really can't eat them?" I say. "Ever?"

"No. I've tried. It makes me feel terrible. Not the food," he adds. "But that she made them for me with the last of her time on earth. Why didn't she want to do something else?"

"She was probably worried about how you'd cope without her."

I think that I might have got the Graham narrative wrong when I entertained it yesterday. What if Graham was a widower? So, married but not married. He could have met Megan because he went to her cottage to order some flies, and then he could have talked to her. She would be a good listener while she was working. She would be sympathetic. Her little shed would have the air of a hushed confessional. That is how their affair could have started.

But then why couldn't she simply have married him, if he was available?

And what about Glen of the Fairies?

"Give me a garbage bag," I say to Paul.

I pile the trays of food into the plastic sack, trying not to examine the contents of the segmented containers. But it's hard not to look at them. "Wednesday" is cabbage rolls. "Friday" is slices of beef, mashed potatoes and peas.

"Okay." I shut the freezer door. "Come on."

"The animals," says Paul, weakly.

"Don't worry," I say. "Nothing's going to eat them. They're not going out as garbage."

I march out onto the back deck, then down the steps and onto the parched grass. The dog clambers out of the reeds when I get to the dock, follows me to the end of the platform.

I lean into the bag, pull out one of the trays. The coolness of the frozen metal feels good against my hand.

"Last chance," I say, holding it out to Paul, who has appeared behind me.

"Go ahead," he whispers, and I reach my arm around to get a good arc and let it fly. It spins above the water, catching the sun and flickering wildly before skidding across the lake and sinking unceremoniously out past a clump of weeds.

The dog, excited by this activity, jumps into the water and paddles around in circles, barking, as I launch each successive tray off the end of the dock.

When the last container of frozen dinners has disappeared into the water, the dog climbs out at the shore, shakes herself vigorously and gets back to her job of hunting frogs.

Paul takes the empty garbage bag from me as we step off the dock. We're quiet as we walk back across the lawn.

"The next part of the fly is the body," he says, as we're climbing the stairs to the deck. "Ostrich herl and guinea fowl feathers. You should find that marginally easier than the tail."

13.

WHAT DO WE OWE THE DEAD?

Should we eat their meals?

Remember their last words, their birthdays and death-days?

Should we take up the hobbies they abandoned? Read the books they never finished? Should we listen to their music and wear their clothes? Is it our duty to become a living memorial to those we loved, those who left us by dying? Who left us so bereft by their dying.

There is a myth that says that, although we think about our dead all the time, twice a day they think of us, for a minute's duration. This happens when the clock reads 11:11—once in the morning and once at night. I don't entirely believe this, but I often look at the clock when it is this time, by accident, and I do wonder, and have wondered, if my dead ever think of me independently of this notion. Mostly because I think about them all the time.

The myth likely arose from biblical origins, as the verse of John 11:11 is about Lazarus, who has been dead for four days, and of whom Jesus says: "Our friend Lazarus has fallen asleep, but I go to awaken him." Meaning he will rise from the dead, that death is but a sleep from which the dead may return.

14.

Every spring, I plant a few vegetables in my small backyard. Their success is largely weather dependent, although I have found that green beans are fairly reliable, no matter what. But tomatoes are very susceptible to weather. Last summer was rainy and the tomatoes either rotted on the vines or never flowered. This summer, with the drought and the heat, I have to constantly water everything, but the tomatoes are doing splendidly. I have been picking one or two a day now for several weeks.

But last night, when I let the dog out for her final pee before bed, she started growling at something by the tomato plants. I was afraid it might be a skunk, so I quickly ushered her indoors. In her fairly short life, she has already been skunked twice and quilled by a porcupine four times. My former dog went to the vet exactly three times in her thirteen years—once to be spayed, once to have some teeth pulled near the end of her life, and once to end her life. My current dog seems to be at the vet's at least once a month. Partially, this is because she has a strong prey drive and does not consider her personal safety when she is on the chase. She will crash through bushes and trees, plunge into swamps, leap off walls in her pursuit of a squirrel or rabbit or deer—basically anything that will run away from her. In those moments, she is oblivious to the limits of her own body and often injures herself. The trick is to avoid those situations.

This morning, when I went outside to gather my daily handful of beans and pick a couple of tomatoes, I found that most of the tomatoes had been eaten, chewed through while they were still attached to their stalks. Not nibbled, like a squirrel would do, but bitten into by something with a large and strong jaw. A groundhog perhaps, or a rat? A fox?

Megan Boyd had a family of foxes living under her cottage. A young man who was learning to tie flies from her and would occasionally sleep over at her house remembered the racket they made at night beneath the floorboards. When he asked about the noises in the morning, she said, "It's just the foxes." Her antipathy about killing salmon extended to all animals. She co-habited casually with the wild creatures around her cottage. She always had a dog as a companion. Her shed where she tied flies was papered inside with pictures of dogs torn from old calendars. Her love of animals was the reason why she could not bear to kill fish.

Megan and I have dogs in common.

One of the beautiful things about a dog is that when you get a new one, you forget the pain at losing the old one. My new dog is six years old now, although I still think of her as "new." Her dominant characteristic is her confidence. A confident dog feels on top of life, trots along the trail with a jaunty bounce and her tail in the air. She has dominion over all she surveys and likes to prove this by killing smaller animals. Thankfully, Charlotte is doing this less frequently as she ages, but when she was in her most highly confident stage as a three-year-old dog, walking behind her on a path, I would come regularly upon her victims—a dead snake, dead chipmunk, dead vole, dead frog. Others would no doubt be horrified by my not keeping her leashed at all times. But I admire her confidence. It is a rare thing to be so full of self, and I wanted her to expand into her nature, not be curtailed by mine.

And she stopped the needless slaughter on her own, only occasionally attacking what is in our path, to protect me. As she has aged, she has come to the logical conclusion that it takes more energy to kill something than it does to let it live. She will still give chase, especially if an animal doesn't instinctively flee her presence (squirrels are particularly stupid in this regard), but it's only a half-hearted lunge off the path and then she's back to her usual jaunty trot.

She is confident, but she still has need of me, likes to sleep with the smallest piece of her body touching mine—a single paw, the tip of her tail. We're not alike, but our natures mesh, which is, I guess, why we have an easy camaraderie. I appreciate her confidence, because it's not what I always feel myself, and I think she appreciates that I leave her be, let her mostly live life on her own terms. Or else, she appreciates my appreciation of her—flattered by the flattery. But it doesn't matter. I am grateful for her love, however I have earned it.

What the dog gives me is peace. I follow behind her on our walks and I feel calm in the quiet of the early morning or in the low light of dusk. I am happy, walking through the woods, or across the fields where we sometimes see deer. The dog exists in the moment she is in, and when I am with her, then I can be in that moment as well.

This morning, we went out early, before the heat had started to rise. We went to the woods that border the edge of the city. There was an osprey on a telephone pole by the lake, and three rabbits in the field. Charlotte flushed a family of grouse from a thicket and they rose into the air with such sound and shudder. Frogs hopped over my boots on the parched path, and we saw a family of raccoons sleeping tucked in the crook of a tree. I didn't think of anything but where we were and the constant unfolding of the forest and its inhabitants.

It was a good morning. There aren't many better.

15.

THE FLIES THAT MEGAN BOYD TIED WERE from the Victorian era. They often relied on exotic feathers from the plume trade as part of their makeup. Increasingly during the twentieth century, the practice of killing rare or endangered birds for their feathers was discouraged, and fly dressers began to substitute as various materials became unavailable. There was a move to use the hair from squirrels and deer, the feathers from local pheasants, but Megan was a purist, and when she was no longer able to purchase particular feathers, she simply stopped tying the corresponding fly.

In her lifetime, feathers from the following birds were some that became harder, or impossible, to procure, as the birds themselves became endangered, extinct or protected:

The grey junglecock, also called junglefowl, is found in southern India and Asia and is the wild ancestor of the domestic chicken. It likes a moderate, canopied forest with low grass cover. At night, it roosts in trees. Habitat loss and the use of its feathers for fly-tying have contributed to its endangered status.

The junglefowl was first introduced into villages about eight thousand years ago, not as food but as an oracle. Wild chickens were thought to be able to tell fortunes and predict the future, a belief that was also popular elsewhere in the world. The Romans used to take chickens with them to the edge of a battle and, depending on the chickens' appetite, they would predict who would win or lose the battle.

Another odd, though interesting, fact about chickens is that they can recognize up to a hundred different chicken faces, helping them to retain the "pecking order" and to be subservient to the more dominant of their brethren. Also, they seem to prefer good-looking human beings to ugly ones.

The Spey cock, now extinct, was a large Scottish chicken—often weighing as much as ten pounds—bred in the Spey Valley. And the gallina is a small, endangered Asiatic wild chicken.

The cotinga, also known as the blue chatterer,

is a brightly coloured bird found in the tropical rainforests of Central and South America. They eat mostly fruit from high up in the canopy. The males have bright blue and purple plumage and their wings make a whistling sound when they fly. The iridescent blue of their coat is the result of air bubbles in the feathers that scatter the light and make it appear as though the blue is shimmering. Deforestation has resulted in significant habitat loss for the cotinga. A feather from the blue chatterer is the definitive element of the salmon fly that began it all for Megan Boyd, the Blue Charm.

Macaws have seventeen current species, many of them endangered. They gather in flocks of up to thirty individuals, mate for life and can mimic human speech. They can live up to sixty years, but their numbers in the wild have decreased because of illegal trapping for the bird trade—many people are interested in owning parrots—and because of the destruction of the rainforest in which they live. The largest parrot, the hyacinth macaw, has a wingspan of over four feet. For some of the flies that Megan tied, she used feathers from the hyacinth macaw, scarlet macaw and great green macaw.

Another endangered bird whose feathers were once popular with fly dressers is the purple-naped lory, a colourful parrot found in Indonesia and Papua New Guinea.

The great Indian bustard, from India and Pakistan, is a large bird, much like an ostrich. It is one of the heaviest flying birds and thrives on grasslands. It is popular and easy to hunt, which is why it is now critically endangered. Apparently, all parts of the bird are tasty. Also, its habitat is under threat as the grasslands are being encroached upon. Once, the great bustard was considered for the national bird of India but was decided against because of possible misspellings of its name.

The Australasian bittern is another large bird. It dwells in wetlands, making its nests at the edges of swamps. A secretive bird with drab markings, it has mostly nocturnal habits and is the basis for the Australian mythological creature the "bunyip," which is said to hold dominion over the swamps and wetlands, eating any hapless wanderers who cross its path. It has been called the "spirit of darkness and the punisher of all wrong-doers" and has an eerie, booming night call. The bunyip is the only mythological beast to have crossed over from aboriginal lore to enter the mythology of the white European settlers.

The blue bird-of-paradise, lovely to watch in

its natural jungle habitat in Papua New Guinea, has been hunted almost to extinction because of its beautiful plumage.

I wonder if Megan ever thought of the birds when she used their feathers? She would have had whole skins of birds in her supplies, as that was the way fly dressers purchased them. Would she look at the shining blue pelt of a cotinga and imagine that bird flying through the rainforest canopy, or did she separate out the living creature from its material essence—the way she distanced her flies from their purpose in killing salmon?

On a rainy, dull winter day in Megan's shed, the feathers and skins of the dead birds would be the brightest objects in her immediate landscape. If she didn't think about the birds themselves, then she couldn't fail to be influenced by the colourful feathers. Did they cheer her? Was she surprised by the sharp start of colour every time she opened the shed door? When a breeze blew in her open window and ruffled the feathers, did the movement please her, or startle her?

Megan Boyd's work contributed to the decline of certain birds, but she was also a conservationist. She was an energetic supporter of the North Atlantic Salmon Fund, an organization engaged in buying out the commercial fishing licences for the fleets overfishing the North Atlantic salmon stocks, and she often contributed her flies to their fundraising events. Granted, her conservation tendencies had a personal motive, because if the salmon were overfished in the North Atlantic, then the numbers returning to spawn in the local Scottish rivers would be greatly reduced. Less fish in the rivers would equal less fishermen. Less fishermen, fewer customers for her salmon flies.

16.

THERE ARE THREE MAIN QUESTIONS TO consider when beginning a novel: What is the story, whose story is it, and how are you going to tell that story? Of these questions, the third one is the most interesting and deserves the greatest amount of thought.

Most stories have, quite frankly, been told before. Most themes have been touched upon. So, it matters how you choose to tell a story. And it pays to spend a long time trying to figure out what the optimum way to do this is going to be. Often, the first thing that occurs to a writer is just the most overused trope. Turning approaches over, spending days, weeks, months, considering all the elements of your story and how they will best be served, will yield up more interesting options for the narrative.

A few years ago, a novelist wrote a story about a woman in the 1930s who walked from New York to Alaska. A basic travel story, with the journey changing the character fundamentally so that the person who arrived in Alaska was no longer the same person who had left New York City. Most writers would have chosen to tell this story by showing the long, epic walk and its day-by-day progression. But this novelist made a different and more radically inventive choice. She decided not to show the walk at all, but rather to give us the character when she stopped somewhere. The effects of the walk were registered on her body and psyche when she paused for the night, or for a couple of days. Telling the story this way kept the tension up, because only by the pause would you know what had happened on the journey. It was a brilliant lesson in structure, and it was what gave the novel a large readership.

So, how do I tell the story of Megan Boyd? Do I begin with her birth and move forward from there, in a fairly conventional biographical chronology? Do I make jumps in time to increase the drama, because the bare facts of the life aren't very dramatic and drama is what gives a story its fuel? I could do a sort of day-in-the-life approach, because most of Megan's life would be apparent in a single day and it seemed that her days tended to resemble each other (with the exception of Sundays). Or I could section the novel according to the different flies she tied, including instructions for making the fly at the beginning of each of the chapters.

But the trouble with turning Megan Boyd's life into fiction is Megan Boyd herself. She was, while not a recluse, a very self-contained woman who led a very self-contained life. A solitary perspective is difficult to convey—unless the person is insane, or a murderer, or has some very unique way of seeing the world. Novels are inherently social and they depend on relationships, and something also needs to be at stake in the relationship in order for there to be enough tension in the story to carry it for the whole length of a novel. It is not going to be enough to write about Megan's customers, or her many kindnesses to the young and old in the village, or even her country dancing adventures. I need her to have a lover, someone to flex against. I need her to feel vulnerable, to not always be in control. I am going to have to bring back Graham and Evelyn.

17.

I TAKE THE DOG OUT AFTER DINNER, WHEN the heat of the day has subsided somewhat. We stroll through the woods and out onto the strip of grass before the river. There are a few other people walking the path, but just below a small waterfall, a knot of people are gathered together on the riverbank. A police officer is unrolling yellow crime scene tape around the trees.

A teenager rides past me on his bike.

"They found him," he says excitedly. "They found him in the river."

"Who?" I ask.

"The dog walker," he yells over his shoulder, pedalling furiously as he rides off.

And then I see the body of a man at the feet of the people who are gathered on the riverbank. He is on his back, both hands above his head, which is probably how he was removed from the water, carried out by his arms and legs. Someone has thrown a coat over him, but it only covers his head and upper torso. I can see the skin of his midriff. I can see that he only has one shoe on.

"Come on," I say to Charlotte, who has wandered closer to the scene, curious about the group of people by the river. We retrace our steps through the woods, back to the car.

Life is so different from fiction. A random, cruel event can occur in life, coming out of nowhere and surprising everyone. A man can be walking his dog and then he can be dead. A person who was never sick and in the middle of their busy life can suddenly die of cancer. It doesn't matter that it's unfair. People don't get the deaths they deserve. Good people can have bad deaths, because death, ultimately, is not within our control, and this is the most frightening aspect of it.

But fiction can't work like that. A writer must slowly build a story and characters, as though they were making a machine, with each part intersecting snugly, each sentence casting forward to hook onto the next. Once you have created someone, you must lean the way they lean, have the understanding they have, never step outside the limits you have determined for them. You cannot just kill them off with no real warning. It will feel unbelievable to readers and they will stop trusting your story. Fiction is measured and reassuring in a way that life isn't, and perhaps that's why we read it, and also why I write it.

18.

IT RAINS IN THE NIGHT. NOT ENOUGH moisture to do any real good to the plants and trees, but the grass doesn't seem quite so dry when I walk across it on my way to the car in the morning.

I hate how parched the countryside looks on my drive to Paul's. After my brother died, I was so broken open that I thought I could feel the trees reaching and stretching as they grew. Now it seems as though they are curling into themselves, shrivelling away to dust.

Paul is sitting on his front porch when I pull into the driveway of his bungalow. He jumps up when he sees me.

"Greetings!" he says, a bit too enthusiastically. The dog, thinking the bouncy lilt in his voice is meant for her, knocks against his legs, barking with approval.

"Sorry." I grab at her collar. "She thinks that you're really excited to see her."

"Oh," says Paul. He doesn't say anything for a moment. "Do you know everything your dog thinks?"

"Pretty much."

He opens the door for me, and the dog bounds into the house.

"Now she thinks that because you're so glad to see her, she will grace you with her presence this morning. She's kind that way."

"Oh," says Paul again. "Well, I suppose that can't be helped."

"You started it," I say. I am annoyed at his eager welcome, which I know was meant for me. I wish I'd never thrown those frozen dinners into the lake.

The dog moves down the basement stairs with tentative fluidity, like a Slinky. She flops on the floor by my chair, letting out a simultaneous groan and fart as she settles her body onto the cool concrete.

In the basement, I forget my irritation with Paul. I like the look of my Jock Scott in the vise. It's not as sharp as Paul's, but it's not terrible either. We're halfway through and I feel that I am beginning to get the hang of it now.

"How long to tie one in real life?" I ask. "How long would it have taken Megan Boyd to make a Jock Scott?"

"A few hours," says Paul. "But she was probably fairly quick, seeing as that's all she was doing."

"But she might have only tied a half-dozen flies a day?"

"Yes."

No wonder she had a four-year backlog and worked up to sixteen hours a day.

The whole enterprise seems weighted against her. I can't see how Megan could ever get caught up with the demand for her flies. It must have been very stressful to always feel so behind in your work. I have a new appreciation for the singularity of her life and the overwhelming busyness of her days. She probably never expected to become so famous. Did she even like her popularity? Wouldn't her life have been more manageable if she hadn't been so good at what she did? But in one of the photos of her that was in a magazine, she is sitting at her workbench, concentrating on tying a fly, and she is wearing lipstick. She has made an effort for the photographer. So, perhaps, although she didn't love the constant busyness, she did like the attention.

"How's your story going?" asks Paul. He passes me a blue feather.

"Hey, I thought those were endangered and not allowed?"

"It's kingfisher. A substitute for blue chatterer. I would never use a bird that's endangered."

Now Paul sounds annoyed with me.

I take the feather. Even in the grey basement, and under the artificial glow of the desk lamp, the blue is shockingly bright. The Jock Scott has a lot of different feathers, which is why it is such a complicated fly to tie. The wing section, which we are about to embark on now, and which gives the fly its shape, is composed of a marriage of peacock, swan, bustard, florican, golden pheasant, summer duck and mallard feathers. The endangered bustard is being substituted by a snippet of dyed turkey wing.

"Don't you think it's kind of odd, using a bird to catch a fish?" I ask.

"Isn't a fish just another kind of bird?" he answers. "Isn't swimming a bit like flying?"

I hadn't thought of it this way before, but Paul has a point. The overworld and underworld, flight above and below us. There must be so much freedom in both of those realms. Our land-based bodies are so cumbersome and slow, so much more limited.

"You haven't answered my question," says Paul.

"I'm thinking about it."

I'm worried my hands are too sweaty to tie in the delicate piece of kingfisher feather. I wipe my palms on the front of my jeans. Megan used an open lipstick tube to place her feathers on, so that they would be ready for use, held in place by the stickiness of the lipstick, although she would have to wipe any trace of colour from the feather before using it.

"I'm following several different avenues of inquiry," I say, which makes me sound like a TV detective. "The problem is that Megan Boyd was, more or less, a solitary being, and I need her to be in a relationship in order to make a story."

"You don't know that she wasn't in a relationship," says Paul. "Just because she never married or had children."

"Yes, that's the avenue I'm pursuing."

"And there's always the fish," he says.

"What about the fish?"

"Well, she was in relationship to the salmon, because she was fashioning a way to kill them."

19.

IF I BRING GRAHAM BACK, IT HAS TO BE IN A more regular way. He can't merely be a Sunday boyfriend, reached by a long car trip for a few hours of pleasure and company. No, he must be a more integral part of Megan's everyday life. He should live nearby and work as a gillie on one of the rivers. This would give him the means to show up at Megan's shed whenever he needs to order flies for his customers. This would give him a perfectly legitimate cover, because I still think he has to be married. Although, after I'm home from Paul's, I seriously entertain the idea of making Graham a widower, and a recent widower at that.

So, here goes.

Graham comes by in the afternoons usually, while his clients are on an early dinner break. He sits in the corner of Megan's shed, on a rickety wooden chair, watching Megan tie flies. He has brought along his flask of tea and has poured her a capful, but she finds it difficult to pause from the momentum of her work to drink it.

"Once I get going," she says to Graham, "I find it hard to stop."

"You work too hard," he says, which isn't really helpful to Megan, because she knows this already.

So, what can happen on Graham's visits that will keep the thread between them taut and alive? They don't fall so easily into bed anymore, because this isn't a new relationship and for some reason, I can't seem to make it one. No, Megan and Graham have finished with courting. They are familiar with each other now, and it is not that the romance has entirely gone out of the relationship, but it is a more watered-down feeling from what it once was. This is partly because Graham is a familiar figure to Megan, even when the affair was in its first flush. He is a gillie like her father and she understands most of what there is to know about him from this information, from her knowledge of his profession.

I think he tells her stories while he is sitting in her shed, drinking tea and biding his time before he will head back out to the river. He tells her stories of the fish his clients are catching with her lures, or of something unusual that happened that morning, or of the animals he has seen near the water and the kinds of men (for they are mostly men) who have hired him for that particular day.

"Right toff this one," he says. "Wears gloves to fish and all."

"What does he do when he catches one?"

"It's me that takes it off, isn't it? Me that gives the salmon his last rites." Graham mimes bashing the head of the fish with his flask as a stand-in for the traditional "priest" truncheon that salmon fishermen use.

"Careful with your talk of toffs," says Megan. "Don't forget that I know HRH."

And this is true, Prince Charles is one of Megan's customers, and someone who visits her in her cottage, sits in the rickety wooden chair where Graham is now sitting. In fact, when she is older and losing her eyesight, it is Prince Charles who arranges for Megan to see a specialist in London and takes her to her appointment. On Prince Charles's recommendation, when Megan Boyd is fifty-six, she is given a British Empire Medal by the Queen, but Megan writes to the Queen to tell her that she can't attend on the day of the ceremony because she is unable to get anyone to look after her dog. Later, Prince Charles presents her with the medal at his fishing lodge in Scotland.

I've wandered away from Graham to talk about Prince Charles and his friendship with Megan. This is because, really, I don't think there is enough between Graham and Megan. It always feels like an effort to put them together. And here's the thing about writing and love, a thing they have in common: If you have to work too hard at something, then chances are good it isn't working. Love and writing rely on an indefinable energy to keep them going, a momentum that comes naturally and isn't a result of trying too hard. For lack of a better description, it's a kind of "magic," and it's either there or it isn't.

The reason I have to start Graham and Megan in the middle of their affair is because I can't imagine the beginning. I can't imagine the unguarded moment. Or rather, I can't imagine it for Megan.

Graham comes to her shed one day and stays longer than usual. He seems reluctant to leave. He keeps clearing his throat and saying he has to go, but he doesn't go.

Megan is at work while he is there, so she isn't looking at him. If she turns away from her vise, she can see him in the corner, on the chair, but she doesn't often turn away from her vise. She can tie a fly without looking, but it is always easier to look. But finally, she does turn and sees that Graham has his hands up to his face, sees that he is crying.

"What's wrong?" She gets up and goes over to him, puts a hand on his shoulder, and he buries his face against her chest, in the scratchy wool of the jacket that covers the softness of her breasts.

This is Graham's unguarded moment. His wife has died and he is bereft. Megan comforts him. She genuinely cares for him and feels bad that he is suffering. But this is not the same as desire, and this is where the problem lies. I need Megan to feel desire because desire is an engine and will move the story along without effort.

Desire is the increased heartbeat, the slow burn, the sudden flicker of hunger that makes itself known, coming out of nowhere and taking all the oxygen.

Megan comforts Graham, and when he turns his face up to her, she bends to kiss him, and this is where it all begins. But she is feeling sympathy for him, not desire. To feel desire, she has to be a little bit out of control, and I can't imagine she is ever out of control with Graham.

And here, I have to think that her style of dress does matter. It does mean something that she dresses like a man, that she takes the male parts at the country dances. It is not just about ease. It is because she identifies more clearly with the male role, whether she has thought it out or not. And to feel desire for Graham, she would have to be more comfortable in the woman's role, or Graham would have to be a different sort of man—which I don't think, given the time and place, he can be. So, Megan would have to be a more conventional woman. She would have to feel the difference between them, to be excited by that difference, and instead, they are more or less equals. She understands everything about the man and his job, and while she may be delighted with the stories Graham brings to her, I can't see that she is erotically charged by this act. They are friends. If they are ever lovers, it is fleeting and accidental.

So, it's work to keep Graham on that chair in Megan's shed, to think of what stories he could tell her that she would be enchanted by, to think of a way she could respond to him that wasn't purely empathetic. And now, after deciding that I needed to bring him back, I realize that I'm going to have to let him go.

My friend Ruby calls while I'm agonizing over Graham.

"Come to the farmer's market with me," she says. "We're going to get you some food. I don't think you're eating properly."

"I am eating."

"What?"

"Well, fish mostly," I say. "Salmon."

"God," says Ruby. "You're not a method actor."

"Can't I be a method writer?"

"I'm picking you up in ten minutes," she says and puts the phone down. Ruby can be very decisive. Depending on the day, I either love this about her or find it aggravating. Today, I am relieved to be interrupted from my endless considerations of Megan Boyd's imagined love life. I'm out on the lawn before Ruby even gets there.

The farmer's market is crowded and full of wasps. Ruby wades through the wall of people in front of the tables, brandishing vegetables for me to nod or shake my head at.

"Now I'm going to cook for you," she says when she has a bag full of tomatoes and greens.

"That's not necessary."

"Not necessary, but nice perhaps?"

The dog loves Ruby, loves when Ruby comes

to cook for me, because she is a sloppy cook and is always accidentally on purpose dropping morsels on the kitchen floor for the dog to snap up.

"Oh, how clumsy of me," she'll say, letting go of a heel of bread or a nugget of cheese.

I sit on a stool at the counter, drinking a beer and watching Ruby slice an onion. The late afternoon sun slants in at the window and the kitchen glows like a lantern. If Graham were cooking for Megan, wouldn't she feel the same contented happiness that I'm currently feeling? Maybe that would be enough in the end? Maybe she doesn't need to feel desire at all? But shouldn't she have at least felt desire in the beginning of the relationship?

"Why are you so quiet?" asks Ruby, turning from the stove to begin chopping tomatoes. "What's going on in your tiny mind?"

"I'm thinking about which suitor to give my main character. Or more precisely, which suitor to take away from my main character."

"Doesn't it get boring to think about your book all the time?"

"No, actually." The truth is that I am never bored when I'm writing or thinking about writing. "I enjoy the challenge of it. It's like a big puzzle that I have to solve."

"Hmmm," says Ruby, which is a noise that means *she* is bored of hearing about my novel. She works in finance and doesn't see much point in an inner life.

"Oh look, I've dropped a bit of sausage."

The dog looks up at her with adoring eyes.

We eat at the table, something I never do when I'm alone, preferring, or finding it easier, to just have my meals on the couch. But Ruby is a stickler for formality.

"You have to keep practising being human, or else you forget how to do it," she says, putting out the water glasses and the napkins, lighting the candles. "Manners are what keep us civilized."

"And art," I say, because I believe that making and appreciating art is the best thing that human beings do.

"Mostly manners," says Ruby. "Not everyone likes art, but everyone likes the door opened for them. Everyone likes a please and thank you."

I feel buoyed up from Ruby's visit, and after she goes, I sit down to make some notes about love and desire.

I wonder if a lover needs to be the solution to the problem that each person represents, an antidote to them? Because all of us instinctively put up barriers to intimacy. All of us naturally shrink rather than expand. For someone to want to know us and love us, they have to be able to see something about us that we can no longer see for ourselves. It's a kind of X-ray vision. A super power.

Graham, no matter how much I twist and turn his character, will never be that person for Megan. But Evelyn might.

20.

MEGAN BOYD RODE A MOTORBIKE. SHE LIKED speed. She dressed in khakis and roared through the streets of Brora, followed by a gaggle of young children cheering her on. She was, apparently—on the motorbike and in her car—a terrible driver. But "terrible" in this case just means going too fast, taking risks and sometimes crashing.

For years, I also rode a motorcycle, and I know the exhilaration of experiencing the countryside this way. I know the exact pressure that the steady push of air exerts against your body as you sit in the saddle, how the smells of the earth rise up to meet you, and how the temperature of the land you ride through is constantly changing. There is coolness down in the hollows, heat on the hills. There is a beautiful recklessness in surrendering to the lean through the corners, accelerating quickly out of them.

One of the things I used to like when I rode a motorcycle was the notion of counter-steering. This is a method by which you can manoeuvre the bike swiftly around an obstacle—to be used in emergencies, if a deer steps into your path, or there is debris or a pothole on the road. You press down on one side of the handlebars, and the front wheel pivots either left or right and then is brought up in the opposite direction by the motorcycle's natural inclination to remain upright. It is a quick way to avoid hazards by relying on the bike's balance, and it works in opposition to how you think it should work. For example, if you want to avoid a pothole, you head directly for it and, at the last minute, put pressure on either the right or left handgrip and the bike will deke around the pothole.

I was taught counter-steering by an older friend I would sometimes go riding with. I wonder who taught Megan how to ride? And I wonder how good a rider she really was, if she knew about such things as counter-steering. She got her bike during World War II and kept it after the war was over. It was standard army issue, a BSA, which was also the type of motorbike my father once rode.

Decommissioned bikes went cheap after the war.

My father rode his bike during his youth in England, around the same time as Megan Boyd. He had worked picking peas for two summers as a young man, saving up to buy the BSA, which he crashed pretty soon after buying it. He broke his pelvis, some ribs and his left baby finger. The finger was badly crushed, and the doctors removed the joint closest to the fingernail. I remember how that finger didn't move as easily as the others on my father's hand. I can still imagine his hands, and it seems to be a fact of death that while the dead no longer have bodies, the living can recall the details of their absent bodies clearly.

Just like lovers can be the cure for each other, Megan Boyd's need for speed was in opposition to the quiet, steady work of tying a salmon fly. I can imagine that her energy was stoked up during those long hours of sitting still in her fly-tying shed, and that when she was finally able to take a break, she charged out of that shed, changed quickly into her riding gear—for she continued to wear army khakis even after the war was over—stomped down on the kick-start of the BSA and fishtailed down the country lane and out onto the main coastal road. There would have been the smell of the salt water and the blur of roadside vegetation, the texture of the road's surface, experienced as tremors through the bike's frame and Megan's body.

Where is Megan going?

While working on a magazine piece about Megan Boyd and her salmon flies, the interviewers for the article had invited Megan to have dinner with them that evening at the local hotel where they were staying during their time in Brora. They received a phone call while they were waiting for her there to say that she would be late because she was helping a friend with her mousetraps.

Evelyn leans against the door frame of her farmhouse, watching the cloud of dust that is Megan's motorbike get closer. There is something so satisfying about watching your lover move towards you, and Evelyn likes to see Megan arrive, partially because it is often dramatic, but also because she wants to savour the moments before they are together, because she has thought about these moments so often and for so long.

Evelyn's husband is at work in a neighbour's field and won't be home until the evening meal. Her children are at school. The house is quiet and peaceful and will be hers alone for the next few hours. She had wanted to wear her new dress, put on a bit of lipstick, but Evelyn also knows enough not to draw attention to the day, not to mark it as special or different from any of her other days.

She has tried to break with Megan. They have tried to call it off. But each time, one of them relents and they exchange meaningful looks while at the butcher's, or they partner up at a ceilidh, even after they tearfully vowed never to do it again. The trouble is that Brora is too small a place not to run into each other somewhere, and so, even when they are on the outs, they are also constantly looking for each other. The only real solution would be for one of them to move away, and that is not going to happen any time soon. Really, they are back together again because they simply can't stand to be apart.

Megan roars into the farmhouse yard a little too fast and skids to a stop just short of the roses. Slapping the dust from her khakis, she lurches off the bike.

"Got them," she says, patting the front of her jacket, where she has stuffed the mousetraps.

When she rips off her goggles, there are rings around her eyes, making her look like some exotic jungle animal. There is dust in her hair and she smells like gasoline as Megan leans into Evelyn, neither kissing nor embracing, because neither is allowed, but her body wants to be close to Evelyn's and her approach is one of instinct rather than sense.

"Not here," hisses Evelyn, grabbing Megan by the lapels of her jacket and hauling her into the farmhouse, kicking the door shut with her foot. They wrestle for a moment in the front hall, trying to kiss or avoid kissing, their bodies suddenly burdensome and unfamiliar after so many days apart.

While Megan was seated on her motorcycle, the angle of her body kept the mousetraps secure beneath her jacket, but now that she is standing in the front hall of the farmhouse, the traps start dropping out from under her clothes, one by one. The women giggle and bend over to retrieve the traps, their heads banging together with their nerves and clumsiness. But then they are kissing and everything is all right again. The world has adjusted to include this, adjusted to include them.

They pick up the traps. Megan follows Evelyn into the kitchen. She has not been in the farmhouse before, and she is eager to be in Evelyn's home, to see where Evelyn spends her days.

The kitchen, even though it is the family gathering place, is also the space that most belongs to Evelyn. She prepares food here, washes up, sits at the big wooden table, drinking tea and listening to the wireless in the evenings.

"I had my last baby on this table," she says to Megan as they enter the room. This is actually not a detail that Megan cares to hear, so she doesn't reply. She mostly tries to think of Evelyn as separate from her family, because to think of her as securely attached to them means that she also has to think about what she and Evelyn are doing as a trespass on that family.

"Where do you want me to set the traps?" she says, suddenly businesslike.

"Under the sink to start." Evelyn puts a hand on Megan's arm. "Sorry," she says. "It's just that everything's mixed up together here. I don't know how to keep it separate."

Megan gets down on her hands and knees. "Do you have a bit of soft cheese?" she says.

She baits the traps under the sink and then they move into the parlour to set traps behind the bureau.

On top of the bureau is a framed photograph from Evelyn's wedding day. She looks so young and beautiful, all smiles outside the church, her arm linked in her young husband's, flowers in her hair.

"Oh, God," says Megan. "You look so lovely." She studies the photo. "And you look so happy."

"I was happy." Evelyn shifts uneasily from foot to foot, a habit left over from childhood when she was trying to keep her feet warm on cold mornings in the milking barn. "But couldn't I be happy now with you and happy then? I was only twenty-two in that life. Just starting out."

"Yes. Of course." But Evelyn's early happiness has thrown Megan. It's not that she can't believe it was true, but she hadn't expected the evidence to be so powerfully moving. "You're so lovely," she says again.

The house is a minefield. There are details everywhere of Evelyn's marriage and family life: a child's marble under the bureau, the weekly wash folded in a wicker basket on the stairs.

Megan can't bear now to go upstairs and see the bedroom where Evelyn sleeps with Dan, has slept all these years with Dan. She shoves the remaining mousetraps at her lover.

"You'll have to do the rest," she says. "I have to meet some toffs at the hotel for dinner."

Evelyn takes the traps. It was only a pretext anyway, having Megan come over to help her set them. She is perfectly capable of catching mice herself and has done so since she was a little girl.

"Will I see you later at the dance?" she asks, for there is a ceilidh tonight at the village hall.

"Yes, yes, I'll be there." Megan pushes past Evelyn in her hurry to get to the front door. No stopping for a kiss. No sweet words. She can't get out of the farmhouse fast enough, rushing into the yard and climbing aboard her motorbike. She's half-way down the lane, tears streaming from her eyes, before she realizes that she's not really crying, she's just forgotten to put her goggles on.

Because here is the secret to Megan Boyd. Here is the kernel at the heart of her, what I have learned from these weeks of thinking so much about her. She cannot connect one thing to another. She cannot see that the salmon fly will kill the salmon. She cannot fully comprehend that having an affair with a married woman means that there are a whole set of people who can potentially be devastated by this affair. Megan knows that Evelyn is married, but she never thinks of Evelyn's family.

Megan exists in moments. This is why she is fundamentally a happy person and well liked by all the villagers and by those who travel to Brora to buy her salmon flies. She fully inhabits the moment she is in and then moves on to the next moment. She doesn't consider the long game. She doesn't dwell on the consequences of her actions.

This would make it seem as though Megan is

simplistic, childlike, but it isn't like that at all. She has trained herself to be the way she is by the type of work she does. We all become what we do. It's inevitable. How could we expect Megan Boyd's character to be separate from the repetitive actions of her daily life?

Megan sits at a kidney-shaped desk in a tin-roofed shed behind her cottage in Kintradwell and ties salmon flies for fourteen to sixteen hours a day. One fly after another. Some simple and some complex. Thirty minutes. An hour. Two hours. Each fly a process that is entered and then completed, a moment that is rendered, with another moment preceding it and another that follows. How could someone who spends their life—their whole life—like this be able to think long term, be able to exist other than moment to moment, salmon fly to salmon fly?

Living in the moment is supposed to be what we all aspire to. It's how animals mostly live, and they seem fairly contented. It's the leading advice given to dying people—try to live in the moment—because there aren't many moments left to them and if you're firmly planted in the moment you're in, you don't notice the lack of future as much.

But living in the moment has its drawbacks, and Megan is now experiencing one of the major ones.

Relationships are progressive. They move from somewhere to somewhere else and they depend on this momentum. Begin an affair with a married woman and it either has to move towards disclosure or closure. It can't stay where it is. Everything evolves.

So, after she has stopped to put her goggles on, Megan roars down the coastal road towards the hotel and feels the terrible knowledge of Evelyn's family move through her like fear. The hard fact of the family, of that marble under the bureau, the basket of small folded shirts on the stairs, makes her feel as though she has to do something. And what it makes her feel that she has to do is to run away, to leave the family intact and make an honourable exit.

Megan takes a bend too fast and has to put her army-booted foot down hard on the tarmac to avoid skittering into the ditch. She is breathless when she arrives at the hotel bar. Her head is full of Evelyn and she can't remember the names of the men from the magazine. One interviewed her and one took her picture. One had red hair and one was dark.

She finds them at a corner table near the fireplace. They rise together when they spot her hurrying across the floor.

"So glad you could make it," says the ginger

one. "But I'm afraid we're a pint or two up on you at this point."

"Can't drink much anyway," says Megan, sitting down beside the dark-haired man. "I'm on the motorbike. It's trouble enough when I'm not drinking. I went into a patch of thistles last week." She looks at the half-empty pint glasses on the table. "But a short whisky wouldn't go amiss. And we are eating."

The ginger jumps up to get her a drink. The hotel bar is busy, full of people having a bite of supper before the dance tonight. Megan recognizes many of the patrons. She'll have to eat quickly, then go back home to feed her dog and let him out before she heads over to the village hall. It's all a bit tight today, and there is always that pile of orders on the shelf behind her desk, growing higher with each passing day. Not to mention the notebook and pencil on the bench outside her door. Every time she leaves the house, at least three people drop by to write down requests for salmon flies in that notebook. She will never get caught up. And that is a truly terrible feeling.

The ginger comes back with her whisky.

"It's hopping in here tonight," he says.

"There's a ceilidh."

"Too bad we're on the 8:00 back to London," says the dark-haired one.

Damian, thinks Megan. That's his name.

"Yes, that's an awful shame, Damian," she says. But she doesn't think it's a shame at all. She would hate the magazine men to show up at the ceilidh. It's one thing to have them poking around her work shed, but quite another to have them gawking at the village dance. They are probably both terrible dancers and would spend their time sneering at the locals to make themselves feel better about their inadequacies. Megan has seen their kind before. There are always men like this at the dance competitions at Inverness. Forced to be there because their wives are competing, but dismissive of the whole enterprise.

Is Dan like that? Evelyn's husband has never attended a dance. Evelyn said he has no interest in it, but if he did come, would he lean against the wall, smoking and sipping his pint, making fun?

It's an awful thought. Megan takes a gulp of her whisky.

"We should have a proof of the article by the end of next week," says the ginger. "We'll send you one. You might like to have the extra photographs for your scrapbook."

"Yes," says Megan. "Thank you." She doesn't have a scrapbook, can't tell if he is mocking her or not.

They had come to her cottage yesterday afternoon. She made them tea. She had put on lipstick to have her picture taken. They laughed at her little dog sitting on a stool beside her in the shed, watching her tie flies.

"We must have a photo of that," said the ginger.

They laughed. They were friendly. They wanted her to like them for the afternoon they were there so they could get the best story out of her. Megan is no fool. She knows how these things work. And yesterday afternoon, she did not begrudge them any of it. But tonight, she wonders why she has agreed to have dinner with them at their hotel. Because these men are not her friends. They do not know her at all, even after asking her all those questions and watching her tie a Jock Scott and a Popham. *Journalists are all about what they've learned that day.* Someone said that to Megan once. She thinks it might have been HRH.

"I'm sorry." She stands up. "I can't stay for dinner after all. I have to get home and see to my dog."

She bolts from the bar, not waiting for their well wishes and goodbyes. The BSA is still warm from the ride in. Megan holds a hand above the engine, feeling the rise of heat from the cylinder. Sometimes on the cold days, she rides with one hand on the handlebars and the other one held above the engine block like this to warm it.

The cottage is drafty. The dog barks his disapproval at being left alone for so long. Megan slaps a bowl of food down on the tiles, closes the windows in the kitchen and the parlour. There's leftover shepherd's pie in the larder. She eats it cold, standing up at the sink, looking out the window to the flat of the North Sea, lying like a grey shelf beyond the garden.

As she's standing there, she feels something on her body, a tug near her waist. Looking down, Megan sees that there's a mousetrap clipped to the hem of her khaki jacket.

She changes for the dance, shedding her khakis for a man's shirt and tie, and a tweed skirt. She had planned to take the car, but when she gets out to the yard, the motorcycle engine is ticking softly, losing its heat and sounding like an insect in the darkness, like a living thing. So, Megan takes the motorbike, even though it's a bit awkward to ride in the skirt.

The village hall glows at the end of the lane, all the lights on and the doors wide open. Megan parks the bike under a tree, leaves the goggles dangling from the handlebars. She smooths down her skirt on the walk across the dirt.

Evelyn is not in the hall, and Megan pretends not to care, dances the first few dances with gusto. She is a very good dancer. It was not something she ever did as a child, she has come to it late, but she is one of the best dancers in the area, can glide effortlessly across the floor. Consequently, she is popular at the dances and is never without a partner.

Evelyn shows up just before Megan's favourite dance of the night and the one she is best at: Machine Without Horses. So, they are able to dance it together, and despite her earlier ambivalence, Megan is glad about this.

Machine Without Horses refers to a steam train and is a dance from the eighteenth century, when the steam train made its first appearance. The dance, a thirty-two-bar jig for four couples, has a pattern of circles and lines, a loose interpretation of the wheels and tracks of the train. The couples move down the floor, circling right and then left with the couples on either side of them, then breaking apart and moving on to take up a new position. Eventually, the first couple ends up as the fourth couple.

Megan likes to start at the head of the line, as part of the first couple. It makes her feel like everything is in its proper order if she can begin there and end up in the place of the last couple, her small journey made and completed. She likes the combination of both the circular and the lateral movements and the constant motion satisfies her need for speed. Sometimes, in the twirl and the flourish, Megan feels like she is flying.

While it did not work for her to be in Evelyn's farmhouse earlier that day, this moment in the middle of the dance is where Megan has dominion. This beautiful, shifting, lively moment is where she shines, clasping hands with Evelyn and swinging her right, then left, letting the music lift her and set her down. There is a pattern to follow and it is a sublime pattern, both the same and different with every rotation. Even though she has performed this dance hundreds of times, it always feels fresh to Megan. It always feels new, and she is new inside it, a blur of legs and arms, her muscles sure of themselves, moving confidently inside the music, the way she imagines the salmon feel, socketed into the rivers that have called them home.

Afterwards, she takes a break, because Machine Without Horses is such an exhilarating dance for Megan that she needs some space between it and the next dance she enters. She likes to still feel the residue of it in her body for as long as it will linger.

She goes outside, lifts her face to the night sky, listens to the sound of her own breathing and the bright strains of the fiddles from inside the hall.

"You left in a hurry," says Evelyn, suddenly beside her at the bottom of the steps. "Today. At my house. You aren't tired of me, are you?" She puts her hand on Megan's arm. "Because I would understand if you were. But I would hate it. So much."

"Evie, I could never tire of you. I just had to go and meet the toffs." The moments of disquiet from the afternoon have long passed, and this moment at the village hall is just glory to Megan. "Shall we leave now?" she says. "We could go back to mine? We'd have an hour."

"Or two," says Evelyn. "Dan will be in bed when I get home. He won't notice the time. Where's your car?"

"I brought the motorbike tonight."

"Did you?" Evelyn loops an arm around Megan's shoulders, bold with the relief that Megan isn't leaving her. "I'm quite partial to the motorbike."

The BSA starts on the first kick.

One of the best things about riding a motorcycle is having someone you love sitting behind you on the pillion, their arms wrapped around your waist, your bodies pressed together, while the headlamp of the bike bisects the night, creates a channel through which you drift past the darkened fields, the shadowy bars of the trees.

Megan drives slower at night. She can't see as well, and she doesn't want to startle Evelyn. Also, she wants to prolong the moment, because it's a very nice one. She leans back into Evelyn. Sometimes, all of life seems miraculous and she is giddy with the surfeit of happiness.

The coastal road is empty and the moon is up, so the sea sparkles on their right and looks more animated than it does in daylight. There's the smell of the salt air wafting up to them and making Megan think, momentarily, of the salmon out there, feeding on the swarms of krill, the schools of herring.

The low hum of the bike is the only sound in the night, drowning out anything else. Megan shifts down to turn into the lane, and the gears whine in protest, then settle into the new, slower speed.

For a moment, they turn away from the shiny flat of the North Sea, and the inland world is so dark that when Megan stops the bike, she leaves the headlamp on so that Evelyn can get her bearings as she negotiates her way across the rough ground to the cottage.

Here I'm going to leave them, as Megan switches off the motorbike lamp and joins Evelyn inside the gate, holds her hand while they cross the grass. I'm going to leave them before they open the cottage door and the dog shoots past them into the darkness, before Megan lights the paraffin lantern so they can find their way to the bedroom, before they take their clothes off and lie naked together on the bed. I will leave them before their murmured endearments, before the slow dance of their bodies in the act of making love. Let them have these stolen moments of happiness all to themselves.

21.

On my last morning with Paul, I am meant to complete the tying of the Jock Scott, which is good in theory. In practice, the fly looks like such a mess, I can't see how to add to it without making it worse. The feathers are matted together, like the whole thing has been underwater already.

"It's so ugly," I say to Paul. While our flies looked fairly similar near the beginning, his has now far surpassed mine. His feathers are still fluffy and uniform and perfectly placed. His thread and tinsel are wound evenly onto the shank of the hook, not full of small lumps and gaps, like mine.

"I could tidy it up for you," he says, "but then you wouldn't be learning anything."

"Are you tempted to tidy it up for me?"

"Of course," he says. "It's really awful."

We both laugh.

Somehow, I limp over the finish line and complete my version of a Jock Scott. The whole exercise gives me new respect for both Paul and Megan Boyd, which is not a bad thing.

Paul unwinds the vise lever, extracts my completed fly and hands it to me.

"Do I have to take it?" I ask. "It's just going to be a reminder of how bad I was at this."

"Here." He removes his perfect Jock Scott from the vise and gives it to me as well. "Yours will remind you of the effort it takes to do this, and mine can remind you of how it's actually meant to look."

"Thank you."

I like the messiness of the workbench, all the bits of feathers, the bobbins of thread and tinsel. I have to think that Megan also found the ordered disorder comforting. The work of building a fly out of the bits of dead birds maybe felt like she was reassembling the bird, felt constructive and positive. Each lure, made from the parts of other living creatures, became a sort of living creature itself.

"Did you think about what I said?" asks Paul. "About Megan Boyd and the salmon? About that being a relationship?"

"I did, actually," I say. "But it would be such a tragic story: the salmon swimming up the river, Megan making the fly in her shed, and then the moment that the salmon is killed by that fly. A kind of inevitable doom. I don't think that's the story I want to tell."

"Yes, I suppose that's part of it," says Paul. "That you have to be comfortable with what you're writing about."

"More than ever," I say. "Like you, I've had a lot of death lately." And experiencing so much death, thinking about it constantly, has made me want to concentrate on life and the living. "I just want to write about something good. It's all I can handle."

"Come upstairs," says Paul, "and I'll make you out an invoice for your taxes."

I already gave him a cheque for the fly-tying lessons at the beginning of the week.

We go into his living room, where there is a piece of paper and pen laid out on the coffee table, ready for this exact moment. I walk over to the fireplace while Paul starts filling out the invoice. On the mantel is a photo of him with his arm around a tall, smiling woman. They are standing in a park. Behind them are benches and trees, the edge of a duck pond.

"What was your wife's name?" I ask. I don't remember this photograph being here the first day I was in the house, the day I was convinced that Paul lived with his elderly mother.

Paul looks up from the invoice. "Sonia," he says. "That was from our honeymoon."

The photo appears to be quite recent. Paul looks no different in the picture than he does now.

"You weren't together long?"

"Three years."

That is hardly any time at all. They still would have been in the first throes of love, full of happiness and plans.

The Jock Scott flies are on the coffee table beside the invoice. From across the room, they look like small birds lying on their sides. It has been nice this week to work on the salmon fly, to build something with my hands and not just with my mind.

"Sonia is a pretty name," I say.

"Yes. She was a nice person." Paul hands me the invoice. "You probably would have liked her. Most everyone did."

I used to wonder where the dead went. I used to think that something of them floated free when they died, remaining with those of us they had left, or lingering in the atmosphere. Now I don't think anything like that. Now I just feel them gone and wish they could come back. I wish this all the time.

But in my better moments, I like to believe that they are full of their days, of the brightness of their days—my father sitting in his deck chair, reading the paper; my friend in her garden—and that they will shed this light, slowly, like fireflies, into the long darkness where they now find themselves.

In the photograph on the mantel, the sun lays down a path through the trees. Everything is so green that it must be spring. The trees have just come into leaf. All that newness that happens every year and makes life so hopeful again.

I feel that I have started at the wrong end of things.

"Maybe I should try and tie some simpler flies," I say. "Easier than the Jock Scott. Do you think that I could have another week's worth of lessons and you could teach me how to tie some beginner flies?"

"I'll adjust the invoice," says Paul, not missing a beat, reaching out his hand for it. I pass it over and watch as he scratches out one number and writes in another.

We don't look at each other, but we're both smiling.

22.

I NOTICE THAT IT'S A LITTLE COOLER TONIGHT when I go out with the dog. Something has shifted very slightly in the air. We have moved deeper into August, and even though the heat is still unrelenting, I can now feel that it will end, that September will come and with it, a release from summer's fever.

I go out to the river, walk along the bank from the small waterfall up to the dam and back again. Soon, the river will be boiling with salmon, but for now, it is quiet. There are a few ducks on the water's surface, some sparrows overhead in the branches of the willow.

We meet George on our way back to the car. He's trotting along beside a tall woman. She has the look of Carlos about her—the same cheekbones, the same dark hair.

Charlotte knocks against George with enthusiasm. She hasn't seen him for a while and is giving him her best, most robust, greeting, the one usually reserved for people who have given her biscuits in the past.

"She likes George," I say to the woman. "She doesn't like many dogs. She's a bit of a snob."

The woman smiles. "George seems to have quite a few friends," she says. "I've been meeting them everywhere."

"I'm sorry about your brother," I say.

"Thank you."

"I talked to him briefly the day before he died. But it wasn't anything important, just the boring things dog walkers say to each other."

"Boring is good," says the woman. "I think that the boring life is probably the best life of all."

"Yes. I do too." I pause, not sure if I should say what I'm thinking, but I do. "What happened to Carlos?"

"I don't really know. We think that George might have fallen into the river and Carlos went in after him and then slipped and hit his head on a rock." She looks down at the ground, and when she looks up again, she has tears in her eyes. "Frenchies can't swim," she says. "Their little dog bodies are too dense. They just sink."

I recall from the news articles that the woman's name is Ana and that Carlos was her younger brother. I know what it's like to lose a younger brother.

The sun has slipped below the tops of the trees, but there's still hours to go before it's dark.

"Shall we walk together for a bit?" I ask. The dogs have trotted up ahead and are companionably sniffing around a garbage bin.

"Yes," Ana says. "I'd like that."

23.

MEGAN BOYD TIED A GREAT MANY DIFFERent salmon flies, but these were some of the ones she tied regularly: Silver Doctor, Durham Ranger, Jock Scott, Thunder and Lightning, Popham, Green Highlander, Snow Fly, Wilkinson.

The "Silver" in the Silver Doctor refers to the tinsel that is wrapped around the shank and forms the body of the fly. Invented in 1850 by the Scottish fly dresser James Wright and very popular in its day, the Silver Doctor is still used and still popular, particularly in Norway and Canada.

The Durham Ranger was also tied by James Wright but was probably invented in the early 1840s by William Henderson, who came from Durham. Meant to be an imitation of a butterfly, the lure contains ostrich and junglecock feathers, kingfisher, blue macaw, blue chatterer and also a twist of black pig's "wool."

Thunder and Lightning was also invented by James Wright and has proven to be one of the best salmon flies in the world, good on almost every type of river, and it's still in high usage today. It was once called the "Great Storm" fly because it was particularly effective on rivers that were naturally dark in colour, and was then only used when the water had risen after a storm.

The Popham—the favourite fly of both Megan Boyd and HRH, Prince Charles—is a complicated pattern that uses seventeen different kinds of feathers, as well as tinsel, silk and thread. The fly was invented in the mid-nineteenth century by Francis Leyborne Popham, from Wiltshire, a racehorse breeder of some renown. His most famous horse was the Epsom Derby winner Wild Dayrell, named after one of Popham's ancestors who had murdered a baby and whose ghost, apparently, haunted the Popham estate.

The green in the Green Highlander comes from seal fur dyed the bright green colour of a Highland tartan. A nineteenth-century fly devised by a Mr. Grant from Wester Elchies, it is a derivative of the Highlander salmon fly and was used to fish on the River Ness, which runs into Loch Ness.

The Snow Fly is an early salmon fly that is distinguished by four tufts of pig's wool set along the shank, each one dyed a different colour. The wool makes the body of the fly very strong so that it can resist the teeth of the young spring salmon and they cannot easily tear it apart.

The Wilkinson was first tied by the Reverend P.S. Wilkinson for fishing on the River Tweed in 1850. It is a salmon fly designed for overcast days, with the brightness of its colours—silver tinsel shank, magenta and light blue hackle feathers—being attractive to the fish in the low light.

In her long career, Megan Boyd had requests from all over the world to make flies that could be framed, often for generous sums of money, but she chose instead to make salmon flies for the fishermen who lived nearby or came up to Brora to fish the rivers during the salmon runs. She was not interested in tying flies to be works of art. She made her flies to be used.

Megan's preferred flies to tie were "attracter" flies. Unlike "imitator" flies, which are designed to imitate insects, the "attracter" isn't made in the image of anything, but it still appeals to a fish's curiosity.

It's an act of translation, taking something that exists and recreating the elements of it to entice the salmon; remaking an insect, or forming a lure that appeals to the memory of the fish.

Megan Boyd also invented a fly, called, of course, the Megan Boyd. It is a small, low-water fly, known as a "shrimper," that is able to attract salmon at the height of summer, when they aren't taking any other flies. Many fishermen called it their fly of last resort. The predominant aspect of the fly is the lovely golden pheasant feathers that form the "topping." They look like butterfly wings and have a rich orangey colour with black stripes near their tips. Underneath them, on the shank of the hook, and as the "hackle," are blue seal fur and blue junglecock feathers. The blue colour is reminiscent of the blue in the first salmon fly that Megan Boyd ever saw, the Blue Charm, given to her by her father.

24.

WHAT OF THE PACE OF THE STORY, THE SPEED at which it is told?

Pacing in a novel is both natural and deliberate. On a basic level, the rhythms of the author's body influence the way a story is told. Where a sentence pauses is often where the writer takes a breath, and this alignment of language with the body operates beneath the layers of story, in the syntax of the words themselves, and in the placement of the punctuation.

But on top of that is the pacing of the story that the writer has put in play. It is wholly deliberate and corresponds to the events taking place within the narrative. When a scene is lingered over, it is because it is important to the characters or the development of the plot. When moments are rushed, it is because they can be. This is the writer telling the reader that while the sequence of events matters, none are important enough to the story to examine in detail.

Because Megan's life wasn't packed with incident or travel or scandal, the drama will have to be helped by giving the whole story an extremely fast pace, having it race along, thus making it seem more dramatic than it actually is.

There is another question to ask yourself when you set about writing a novel, perhaps the most important question of all: Why? Why do it? The world does not really care that you tell this particular story. There are always plenty of other stories that can be told, ones that are more interesting, more politically or socially relevant. Stories that address the moment of time that we stand on and therefore have greater imperative.

It is hard to write a novel, to make something out of nothing. And it gets increasingly harder, not easier, the longer I do it. I find more challenges with writing now than I faced when I was younger.

So why do it? Why tell the story of Megan Boyd? She had her measure of fame, has gone down in the history of fly fishing as one of the great salmon-fly dressers. So, I am not rescuing her from obscurity.

In fact, my version of her story might be a distortion of her life rather than an unveiling. I have only the scantest of facts to go on and I have made decisions based on these facts, which may or may not be correct. It could be that I am actually doing her memory a disservice in my treatment of it.

But this is what I know about death: It reduces the most complex of human beings to the lowest common denominator. All the particularities of a person, all their rough edges, are smoothed over after they have died. All is forgiven and all is forgotten. The living really have no time for the dead, and it is easier to file them away with a couple of clichés than it is to continue to engage with their intricacies when they are no longer there to participate actively in this engagement, to push back against your version of them.

Megan Boyd's manner of dress, her motorcycle riding, her living alone in a bare-bones cottage have been reduced to the adjective *eccentric*. Because she never married or had children, it is assumed she never had a relationship. Her life has been whittled down to the facts of her work, to her accomplishments in this arena.

But what of how she felt? What of her thoughts? What of her experiences in her own skin?

It may be that I get most things wrong in this novel, but if just one scene, one line of dialogue, moves the reader to consider Megan Boyd not merely as an oddity but as a fully realized human being, then I have done my job as a novelist. Because to really understand someone, we have to be moved by them. And to be moved by someone is to feel empathy for them, and this is what joins us to the rest of humanity. Feeling that we belong to humanity and behaving with compassion towards our fellows is perhaps the most important responsibility of being human today. So, it matters to be able to relate to anyone whom we consider to be "other."

All of my recent deaths have made me think a lot about life, about what makes up a life and how it is judged. Are the living merely trudging through a succession of days—the "petty pace" as Shakespeare called it—made up of routine and ritual? Is the worth of a human life determined from the quality of relationships or the usefulness of work? When we look back on our own lives, what do we see? Does the endless procession of days shrink to the handful of moments when we have felt the strongest emotions?

I am telling this story for these reasons and also because it is a story I feel able to tell. All writers need to feel equal to their material before they are able to render it effectively, and all writers are limited by themselves in this regard—by their own histories, likes and dislikes, personalities, prejudices and their abilities as a writer. Just because you are a writer doesn't mean you can write about anything. It won't be convincing if you don't have points of connection with your subject matter. I feel able to tell this story because I have several points of connection between myself and the character, and because the small canvas of the subject matter is suited to my natural abilities as a writer. I am not the teller of huge sagas that span centuries. I am someone who does best when writing about a closed world.

When I think about Megan Boyd now, I am thinking about her sitting in her tin-roofed shed, tying salmon flies from sunrise to sunset. I think of her working. I think of her being happy in her work, the way that I am mostly happy in mine. At the end of the day, as she walks from the shed to her cottage, I imagine she feels the satisfying exhaustion that comes from spending oneself at the work one was designed to do.

When I have been writing well, productively, I reach the end of the day having run out of words, having been wrung out of words, having used them all up. This often makes me a terrible companion in the evening, as I literally have nothing to say, or nothing left to say. But instead of rendering me empty, this lack of language, this feeling that I have used all the words I had in me that day, makes me whole again.

I have reached the place where I can begin. I know enough about Megan Boyd now to start writing her story. This note-taking can come to an end.

To avoid upsetting any of her relatives or friends who might still be alive, I will change Megan's name.

All the things that kept me company during this part of the process have to fade into the background now, or be folded, delicately, into the mix of the story, so delicately that they will be invisible to the reader. Aspects of my dog can become aspects of her dog, thoughts about my dead can double as her thoughts, but it must be done so subtly as to be unnoticeable. I need to become Megan Boyd, and in doing so, I need to leave myself and my world behind. Whatever is preoccupying me at the moment needs to be synthesized into fuel for the narrative, but it has no place in the actual narrative. This is the sleight of hand that comes with writing a novel. It is all about making yourself disappear.

The weather has broken, for a day at least. It has cooled and the sky is grey. There is a breeze and the smell of rain in the air. I woke in the night to hear its whispers on the roof. It is just a matter of time before it begins again.

Part Two

Blue Charm

THE CURTAINS DRIFT ON THE BREEZE FROM the open window, listing over Ruth's crib. She raises her hand towards the movement, trying to catch the shadows of the birds lifting and lowering from the branches of the oak beside the house.

This is her earliest memory. All through childhood, it rests just beneath the surface and she can haul it into consciousness at will. When Ruth becomes an adult, the memory vanishes, disappearing under the accumulation of other memories, but she never forgets the feeling of it, and sometimes, this is what surfaces still, the sensation of reaching for something that cannot be grasped.

Ruth is born at the end of January in 1915, in Walton-on-the-Hill, Surrey, a scattering of houses on the edge of the North Downs, with a large pond at the centre of the village and a history that dates back to the Romans. Her father, Arthur, is in France, fighting, when Ruth is born, her consummation his last act before leaving for the front.

When Arthur returns at the end of the war in 1918, he has never met his third child, even though she is three years old at this point.

Before the war, Arthur worked as a chauffeur for one of the large estates in the area, but crouching in the narrow, muddy trenches in France has left him with a loathing for small spaces, and when he returns to England, he can no longer bear to be trapped inside a car or a house. He feels better outside, in the open country, so he follows up on a contact from one of his fellow soldiers and takes a job as a gillie in Brora, Scotland.

Ruth's sisters sob on the train northward. They will miss their friends, their school, the pond in the village where they sometimes see swans and always ducks. Ruth's mother, Annie, doesn't cry but feels much the same as her two eldest daughters, for many of the same reasons. Only Ruth and her father are excited by the adventure. Ruth is too young to have real attachments outside of her family, and Arthur is hungry to make a new life to match the new person he wants to become after fighting in the Great War.

When they cross from England into Scotland, Arthur holds Ruth up to the train window, so she can see what he sees, the undulation of hills, the long stretches of heath.

"Nothing but blessed space, Ruthie," he says.

The cottage that comes with the job of gillie is small and cramped, low-ceilinged and dark. It is not as nice as the house they left in Walton-on-the-Hill, and Annie knows this immediately and has to work hard at not resenting it. She sets about trying to make the rooms habitable, sends the older girls out to pick flowers for the kitchen table and bedrooms.

Arthur doesn't really care about the cottage. Being indoors is just a kind of sufferance until he can be outside again. He hoists Ruth onto his shoulders and strides off in the direction of the river.

Ruth holds onto her father's hair, which he usually minds and stops her doing, but today he doesn't care. He quickens his pace on the downhill slope, stones skidding under the soles of his boots.

The river is dark and twisty, littered with rocks and backed by a line of hills. Ruth remembers the village pond, its smooth surface reflecting the overhanging trees, the gentleness of it. But this water is nothing like that water. The river moves, pulling itself along, arching over a small waterfall, then spiralling out into a shallow pool, where it gathers its strength to pounce again.

"Look at that, Ruthie," says Arthur. "Look at the magnificence of that."

At the river's edge, Arthur lowers his daughter onto a rocky ledge, removes his shoes and socks, then hers, and wades out into the water, pulling Ruth with him. The water is cold and the stones wobble under her feet. She can feel the river current nosing her legs like the snout of a dog.

When they get back to the cottage, Annie has the bedding airing in the yard, has the cooker going and a pot of tea on the table with a plate of the special Christmas biscuits. Eliza and Marjory have claimed the bigger bedrooms, leaving Ruth with the box cupboard at the top of the stairs.

The cottage is furnished, but Annie has nothing but complaints about what has been left to them.

"The blankets are full of moths," she says to Arthur. "The fireplaces haven't been swept out. All the crockery is chipped. There's no coal for the cooker. I had to use sticks from the yard. Two of the windowpanes upstairs are broken."

"The river, Annie," says Arthur, grabbing a fistful of biscuits from the table. "It's a real thing of beauty." He passes a biscuit to Ruth, who is holding onto his trouser leg, trying to stretch herself up to table height.

"The house is a disaster," says Annie.

Arthur and Annie stare at each other across the table. Ruth knows that her mother is unhappy. She has seen that look before. She tightens her grip on her father's trouser leg and nibbles at the chocolate covering on her biscuit, pretending to be a mouse. The cuff of Arthur's trouser leg is wet from when they were standing in the river. It is cool where it touches the skin of her calf.

The box room slopes down on one side, but Ruth can stand upright in the junction of roof and wall, so it isn't an impediment. It makes the room feel normal sized, made for her. She is not stopped by the roofline. The window opens to the hills, soft and low, burnished with the last of the evening sun.

The bed is hard. The pillow smells like bad breath. The summer dark, when it comes, is absolute. Ruth can't even see her hand when she raises it in front of her face. But if she turns onto her side, she can watch the stars criss-crossing the heavens, and the bright coin of the moon in its pocket of darkness. She is almost scared, but not quite, and can hear the low murmur of her parents' voices in the next room. She puts a hand on her leg. The skin still feels cold from the water of the river.

School is torture. The girls gather together like birds in the yard, squawking over every shiny thing. The boys are loosely attached to a football, unravel from it along the weedy edges of the school field.

Ruth plays an invisible game with stones. She counts to a thousand, forwards and backwards. She keeps on the move, shuffling along the walls of the school, then arcing out into the field. If she stands still, then the other children will know that she is without friends, but if she keeps walking, it won't be so obvious. She won't be called out.

Inside, she is bored by the Kings and Queens, is good with numbers, likes the memorization of poems, the way the words bounce around in her head, bumping up against each other, like fruit rolling in a wooden bowl. *How pleasant thy banks and green valleys below, / Where wild in the woodlands the primroses blow.*

When the bell rings, Ruth is out of the building and running down the lane, her cardigan unbuttoned and rising behind her like a cape. She heads not for home but for the river, where she knows she will find her father fishing the salmon pools with a client. If it is a sunny day, she will look for Arthur at the loch, and if it is cloudy, she will search him out at Stoney

Pools. His territory is the south part of the River Brora, running from the loch down to the sea.

Today, Ruth finds Arthur just below Stoney Pools, on his way to the Fannich Pools. He is walking with a client, a tall man in a tweed cap and green wax jacket.

"Daddy!" She calls for him long before she gets to him, likes to watch him turn towards the sound of her voice, see his wide smile.

He waits until she has caught up, puts a hand on her shoulder. "My youngest," he says to the tall man. "The keeper."

The man nods to Ruth. "Help your father out, do you?" he says.

"She knows the river almost as well as I do." Arthur squeezes Ruth's shoulder. "Tell your mother not to wait tea for me. I'm going to be out here until dark."

Ruth breaks from the men, runs along the bank of the river before heading overland to the cottage. She dodges tufts of heather, pretending that they are rocks and she is a salmon swimming around them. Nearing the cottage, she listens for the sharp bark of the collie, Shep, who always hears her coming, whether through the fields or by road, and comes down to meet her at the gate.

Tea is baked beans on toast, Ruth's favourite. She eats alone. Annie is darning socks in a corner of the kitchen. Eliza and Marjory are giggling over the pages of a magazine in the sitting room. Their jokes never include Ruth, but she doesn't mind. She likes the background sound of their laughter. It's reassuring, like birdsong.

"I'll feed the chickens, Mummy," she says when she's finished eating, scooting off her chair and pocketing the last bit of crust for Shep, who isn't allowed indoors and sleeps on a bed of straw in a little wooden house near the hens. At ten, Ruth is still small enough to be able to squeeze through the door of Shep's house and likes to go outside and lie with the dog sometimes after tea. It is surprisingly comfortable on the straw, curled up against the warm, friendly body of the collie.

Shep gently takes the scrap of toast from Ruth's hand, trots after her as she fills the tin pail with grain and walks down to the end of the garden where the chickens live in their wood and wire prison. Ruth scatters the feed from the pail, then bobs her head in imitation of the birds pecking at the ground. She runs round the outside of the enclosure, being a chicken, Shep at her heels.

Arthur isn't home when Ruth goes upstairs to

bed, and she listens for the click of the gate, the fall of the latch on the kitchen door, but drifts off to sleep before she hears either sound. She wakes to a small knock on her bedroom door.

"Ruthie?" The door opens. "Did I wake you?"

"No," Ruth lies.

"I have something for you." Arthur comes across the room, bends over Ruth's bed.

Ruth scooches up until she is sitting, puts out a hand.

"Mind, it's sharp." Arthur places the salmon fly in his daughter's palm. "It's called a Blue Charm. Good for low water."

In the dim light of the bedroom, Ruth can't decipher the details of the lure, but she can feel the softness of the feathers, the sharp spike of the hook.

"Is it really blue?" she asks.

"Like a piece of the sky." Arthur lifts the fly from Ruth's hand and places it gently down on the little table by her bed. "I'll put it here and you can have a good look at it in the morning." Ruth slides back down in her bed, and he pulls the covers up to her shoulders, leans over to kiss her on the forehead. "Good night, Ruthie."

"Good night, Daddy."

In the morning, Ruth inspects the Blue Charm, running her finger lightly along the top feather and the bright blue hackle. She holds it up to the window and the sun catches the brightness of the blue and makes it sparkle. Turning it over in her palm, Ruth examines the layer of thread that winds around the shank. The fly is so pretty, like a small bird, like the picture in her mother's room of a tiny bird stalled at the throat of a flower.

Arthur isn't much good at tying flies, but his friend Richard is. Richard is a fellow gillie on the Sutherland estate. He works the upper reaches of the River Brora, and it was he who tied the Blue Charm that Arthur gave to Ruth.

"You're young to learn," he says, when Ruth proposes the idea to her father, and Arthur presents it to Richard.

"I'm a good learner," says Ruth. "I can multiply anything, and I know all the words to 'Sweet Afton' and 'A Red, Red Rose.'"

She stands up tall and begins to recite. "*O my Luve is like a red, red rose / That's newly sprung in June; / O my Luve is like the melody / That's sweetly played in tune.*"

Richard holds up his hand to stop Ruth from going any further. "I don't need to hear any more of that bloody poem," he says. "We'll give it a go." He opens up his salmon fly wallet and takes out a Blue Charm, passes it to Ruth. "I want you to take this apart and put it back together again."

Ruth uses the Blue Charm that her father gave her as a model to guide her when she has the lure that Richard presented her with in pieces. He has shown her how to wind thread onto the hook from a bobbin, but otherwise she is without instruction. She crouches at the little table in her bedroom, in the path of the window light, trying not to grip the pheasant feather too firmly so it doesn't bend or clump together.

The elements of the fly, when separated from the whole, look like bits of scrap, like nothing of consequence. A tip of a feather. A fingernail-sized piece of black wool. A bit of tinsel that isn't long enough to drape over a branch on a Christmas tree. But when they are assembled correctly, these scraps make something pretty enough to tempt a fish to leave the river.

"Not bad," says Richard when Ruth presents him with the rebuilt Blue Charm the next afternoon. "Must be your small fingers. Let's try you with something a bit harder." He gives her a Wilkinson.

This time, Ruth doesn't have a model for the fly, so she has to concentrate on the way the lure is put together before she starts to take it apart. She steals a sheet of drawing paper from Eliza and makes a rendering of the fly, labelling where the feathers go, and the wool, and the tinsel and the floss. It's a much more difficult task than the remaking of the Blue Charm, and Ruth is proud of her rendition when she hands it back to Richard the following day.

"Well, well," he says, turning the salmon fly over. "You've done a fine job, little lassie." He digs in his pocket, passes a half crown over to Arthur.

"I had money on you, Ruthie," says Arthur somewhat sheepishly.

Father and daughter walk home together that evening, going through the village so that Arthur can buy Ruth an ice cream from the new Italian shop that has recently opened in Brora.

"It's only fair," he says, handing over the half crown as payment for their two vanilla cones.

They sit outside the shop, on a low stone wall, watching the passing of the horse and carts on their way to and from the salt flats in the harbour.

"Daddy," says Ruth, "what's the hardest salmon fly?"

"What do you mean?"

"The hardest to tie."

"Ah." Arthur thinks for a moment. "The Popham," he says.

Ruth works her ice cream cone, trying both to savour it and not to finish it quickly, two things that operate against each other.

"I'll try that next then," she says. "But this time, Daddy, I think you should bet a pound on me."

School is sufferance, but the school leaving age has been lowered because of the post-war depression, with children needing to work to help their families out, and Ruth escapes the academic world at fourteen. She leaves without a backwards glance, tossing her school books in a hedge as soon as the school building is out of sight.

Arthur has secured her a job, her first real job, refreshing the flies in a tackle box for one of his clients. She works at the family kitchen table after breakfast has been cleared, her mother insisting that she put a layer of newspaper down first.

"We eat here, Ruth," she says.

Annie is a strict believer in not mixing the outside with the inside, although this is a constant battle with her youngest daughter, who tries to fill her bedroom with birds' nests and coloured leaves, stones from the river, the empty husks of insects.

For the rebuilding of the flies in the tackle box, Ruth is paid the generous sum of five pounds.

"That's enough to set you up proper," says Arthur. "Enough for bobbins and skins and a good tying vise."

Ruth has already thought of this, has priced out what she'll need to begin making salmon flies for a living, knows how much of the money she'll have left over once she's purchased feathers and thread, different sizes of hooks.

"I'm going to buy you a new suit too, Daddy," she says.

Arthur has worn holes in the fabric of the one suit he has now. It was the suit he married in and his girth has increased since that time, so that now when he goes to work in it, he can't button up the jacket and the wool strains over his backside when he bends down.

When Arthur goes to London to buy the new suit, he takes Annie with him for the weekend. It is the first time she has been there since they moved north and the visit lifts her mood for weeks to come.

"Just being on the streets with all the people made my heart sing," she says to her daughters when she returns, and Eliza and Marjory are pestering her for details of the fancy clothes in the shop windows. She hums while she cooks the tea, something Ruth cannot remember her mother ever doing, even before they moved to Scotland.

Ruth goes outside. Her father is down by the henhouse, smoking a cigarette. His new suit looks sharp against the boards of the coop, all the colours of the cloth bright and clean.

"You look very smart," says Ruth.

They stand side by side at the end of the garden. Before them is the grassy slope of the river valley, the soft shapes of the hills like fallen horses.

"I couldn't breathe," says Arthur. "It was so noisy. There were crowds of people trapped together, jostling for space. I thought I'd never get out."

Ruth isn't sure if her father is talking about London or the war.

"Well, you're out now," she says.

"Aye."

Arthur takes a pull on his cigarette. Soon his new suit will smell like his old one, of smoke and sweat and fish.

Ruth tugs his sleeve, like she used to when she was a small child.

"Shall we go and show the salmon your new duds?" she says.

Her father laughs. "I'll be surprised if they recognize me."

He grinds his cigarette end under his boot heel and they start down the slope together, towards the river.

Durham Ranger

THE HOUSE CAN'T BE SEEN FROM THE ROAD.

"The longer the drive, the larger the castle," says Arthur, as they walk through the fancy iron gates and past the stone pillars flanking the carriageway.

Ruth, who has polished her old school shoes for this occasion, looks in dismay as the dust from the drive starts to film across the leather.

"But it's not really a castle, is it?"

"He's a Lord, so it might as well be."

The Lord isn't home, but the Lady is. She makes them wait on the steps and then re-emerges in boots, carrying a walking stick, three enormous hounds nudging her heels.

"They're Russian," she says, as though that's meant to explain everything about them.

Arthur worries the brim of his cap in his fingers. "It's very kind of you," he says. "We are very grateful. We are . . ."

The Lady waves her stick to silence him and turns to look at Ruth. Her eyes are bright and close together. She tilts her head slightly, like a bird.

"I've heard you're a very good dresser."

Ruth looks nervously down at her dusty shoes, her ill-fitting skirt, and then realizes what Lady Drummond means.

"Yes," she says. "I can tie a decent salmon fly."

"Decent or good?" The head tilts to the other side. One of the enormous Russian dogs knocks against the back of Ruth's knees and she almost stumbles.

"Good," Ruth says, regaining her balance. "Sometimes very good."

"Then no need to grovel," says Lady Drummond to Arthur. "I will make excellent use of your daughter's abilities. It seems a fair exchange."

"The Lady is a first-rate salmon fisher," says Arthur to Ruth.

"I've had the treble more than once," says Lady Drummond.

Ruth is impressed, despite her nerves. The "treble" is usually only undertaken by men. It refers to the catching of a salmon, the shooting of a stag and the killing of a grouse, all accomplished within a single day.

The cottage is a long walk from the estate, across several fields, up a hill and down the other side. The small wooden gate off the laneway is overgrown with brambles. Lady Drummond slashes at them with her stick to clear a path. She throws open the cottage door with such force that it bangs against the adjacent wall and releases a cloud of dust.

"It's been much neglected and for too long," she says. "I had a gamekeeper in here for a while, but that was years ago now." She strides into the tiny building and Ruth and Arthur bob along in her wake. The dogs stay outside in the overgrown garden, nosing under the hedge for rabbits.

The rooms have cobwebs on the ceiling, peeling paint on all the walls. There are rodent droppings on the small work surface in the tiny kitchen. One of the windows is cracked.

"What do you think?" asks Lady Drummond.

"It's lovely," says Ruth.

The shed next to the little cottage has a corrugated red tin roof and a big window that looks out to the sea. Ruth stands in front of the window, staring at the thin white threads atop the distant waves.

The vista is mesmerizing and she finds it hard to break away when it's time to leave.

"We'll get your mother out here to help make the place habitable," says Arthur, when they're walking home.

"I could live in it now," says Ruth. "As it is. Did you see the view, Daddy?"

"I did. It was entrancing. It's all going to work out splendidly."

But Annie isn't enamoured with the cottage.

"It smells of mould."

When she's shown the shed, she regards the generous window critically. "You'll get a lot of draft through that," she says.

But she stays and helps Ruth sweep out, put a few dishes on the kitchen shelves, lean the mattress up against the outside wall of the cottage to air it out.

Arthur brings over an old dressing table that he's salvaged from one of his wealthy clients, positions it under the window in the shed.

"You can use this as your desk," he says to Ruth. "And I've made you some cubbies to hold your skins and feathers."

Her parents stay until tea time and then they leave Ruth there, alone in her strange new home.

She stands by the gate, watching them lurch away in the horse and cart that Arthur has borrowed for Ruth's moving day. The plume of the horse's tail is all that is visible as they round the bend in the road.

It is not yet dark, so Ruth goes out to the shed, sits at the kidney-shaped dressing table, running her hands over its smooth surface. Tomorrow, she will start, she thinks, but there is her vise on the window ledge, and the new cubbies her father made to the left of her desk are already full of materials. There will be light for at least another hour or so, and Arthur has promised several clients his daughter's exquisite flies for the coming week.

The first fly Ruth ties in the shed is a Durham Ranger. The bright blue of the hackle is cheering and the silver tinsel for the ribs glitters beautifully, caught in a ray of the setting sun. Working on the fly, head bent in concentration over her desk, Ruth can forget the loneliness she feels at being apart from her family for the first time in her life.

Over the coming weeks, Arthur visits often, Annie not at all.

"It's incumbent on you to come to me," she says to Ruth. "Not the other way around."

But Arthur shares none of that Victorian sentiment. He is up at Ruth's cottage every chance he gets, sometimes on the pretext of collecting flies, but often just to have a cup of tea and escape the constant and sharp unhappiness of his wife. He sits on an old chair in Ruth's shed while she works, drinking his tea and talking to her back.

"Honestly, Daddy," says Ruth, after one lengthy recounting of Annie's complaints of him, "why did you ever marry her?"

"I thought we had a great deal in common."

They both laugh out loud, trying to imagine what this commonality might possibly once have been.

Arthur visits on behalf of his clients, but soon, the clients themselves start to come up the coast road to see Ruth, and she has to leave a book and pencil on the bench outside her cottage for the fishermen to write down their orders when she isn't home.

Once in a while, Lady Drummond strides up the drive with her Russian dogs to choose a few flies for herself. She never puts in an order and so Ruth is required to give her flies that she had meant for someone else, and then has to stay up later than she wants to make new ones.

But she doesn't mind. It seems a small price to pay for her rent-free tenancy, and Lady Drummond never takes more than one or two flies at a time. She favours the Durham Ranger and the Jock Scott, so Ruth tries to have several of each always to hand.

The Lady arrives one day and knocks with her stick on Ruth's shed window, startling her.

"Come in," says Ruth, but Lady Drummond remains standing outside the shed, and so Ruth gets up from her chair and goes into the garden.

"I brought you something," says Lady Drummond. She's carrying a basket over one arm. "I thought you might like it." She pulls back the cloth that covers the basket and Ruth looks in to see a squirming black and white puppy.

"The shepherd's collie had nine puppies," says Lady Drummond. "And it occurred to me that you might like the company of a dog, being all alone out here."

Ruth has been feeling lately as though she is never alone enough, what with Arthur's constant visits and the dropping in of the local fishermen, but she doesn't say this. She reaches into the basket and lifts out the puppy and puts him down on the grass.

"I like his white feet," she says. "They're like four little socks."

The puppy wants to chew the legs of Ruth's desk. If a feather falls to the floor while she's working, he runs off with it. In the garden, he snaps the heads on the flowers and rolls in the carcass of a long dead fox. But at night, when he's curled up on the rug in the parlour, she often sits on the floor beside him, stroking his silky fur and listening to the whistle of his breathing.

One day, Lady Drummond arrives in a pony and trap.

"You're wanted at home," she says. "Bring the dog. I don't know how long you will need to be there."

Ruth tucks the puppy under one arm and climbs up into the trap.

"What's wrong?"

The Lady just lays a hand on Ruth's arm and shakes her head.

Arthur is tucked up in bed in his blue-striped pyjamas. He is surprised to see his youngest daughter.

"What are you doing here?" he says. "You're meant to be tying a set of flies for the Duke."

"Arthur, you know very well you're not going back out on the river," says Annie from the doorway.

"Of course I am." He struggles to sit upright but doesn't have the energy and flops back down again.

Ruth sits down on the edge of the bed. She can hear Socks crying out in the yard where she has tied him to a drainpipe. She takes Arthur's hand.

"Daddy," she says. He looks at her with wild eyes, his brow spiked with sweat.

"Help me, Ruthie," he says. "I don't know why they're keeping me here."

Eliza and Marjory arrive by train that evening. They walk from the station arm in arm. Ruth watches them arrive from the bedroom window, can hear their voices drift ahead of them up the road. When they come into the house, she listens to Annie talking softly with them in the kitchen, preparing them.

"We're all here now, Daddy," Ruth says, but Arthur is suddenly beyond hearing. His eyes are closed and there is a lot of time between each breath. Ruth can count to eight, then to ten. By the time her sisters get upstairs, her father barely seems to be breathing at all. She puts her head on his chest, listening to the slow slippage of his heart, the flannel of his pyjamas warm against the side of her face. She hasn't put her head on her father's chest since she was a child. There's such a relief to doing it that she keeps her ear pressed against his chest until there is only silence beneath it, and the patch of flannel against her cheek grows slowly colder.

They dress Arthur in his good suit, comb his hair across the bald patch on the top of his head.

There are to be no shoes in the coffin, but Ruth polishes his brogues anyway and then puts them neatly by his side of the bed. She slips a fly into his breast pocket, a Durham Ranger, the first one she tied when she went to live in the Kintradwell cottage.

"There's unlikely to be fish in heaven," says Eliza, who stands across the room, watching her do this.

"But there might well be people wanting to fish," says Ruth.

It rains at the graveside, great sheets of water running down the earthen walls of the grave and pooling on top of the coffin. Eliza and Marjory share an umbrella and Ruth holds one over her mother. Water drips down the back of her neck. With all the rain, it is hard to tell who is crying and who isn't.

Back at the house, there is tea and whisky and sandwiches. Everyone crowds into the parlour and there is the overwhelming smell of wet wool from the rain-soaked tweed of the mourners.

Ruth is encouraged to see many of the fishermen whom Arthur worked for, but becomes gradually annoyed when some of them use the opportunity of the funeral to order salmon flies from her.

After the last guest has left, Ruth goes upstairs and sits on her father's side of the bed. She touches his pillow, which still carries the dent of his head. Then she bends down and touches the tips of his newly polished shoes, first one, then the other. It's mostly dark in the room, just the borrowed light from downstairs rising weakly up the staircase, and night thick upon the window. She can hear the overlapping voices of her mother and sisters, how similar they sound to each other.

On a nail on the back of the bedroom door hangs Arthur's old suit. Ruth gets up from the bed and walks over to it, burying her face in the worn wool of the jacket, breathing in the scent of fish and smoke, the metallic tang of the river underneath everything, in every fibre of the cloth.

When she leaves the next day, Ruth takes the suit with her. Annie assumes her daughter will be giving it to one of Lady Drummond's shepherds and is grateful.

"Thank you for thinking of that," she says, in a tone usually reserved for Eliza and Marjory.

But Ruth has no intention of giving her father's suit away. She walks back to her cottage, the suit under one arm, Socks tied to a length of rope and trotting along the road in front of her.

She pushes the gate open, flips through the notebook on the bench outside her front door, noting with dismay the number of new orders that have been written there during her absence.

Inside, the cottage is damp. Ruth banks a fire in the grate, puts some food down for the dog. She carries her father's suit to her bedroom, where there is a small mirror overtop of her dressing table.

The trousers don't fit at all. They drop to the floor even when she has buttoned them up. But the jacket is better. She turns back the sleeves, smooths down the lapels with an open hand. In the mirror, she regards herself critically.

Not quite a boy. Not quite a girl.

Her mother's high forehead.

Her father's green eyes.

Thunder and Lightning

Ruth looks out at the horizon, standing at the bottom of the garden, where she has the best possible view of the sea. The sun is barely up and there is just a whisker of light between water and sky to separate night from day. There's nothing out there. An empty sky. The empty sea.

"All clear," she says to Socks, who is snouting through the flower bed, following the scent of night rabbits.

Ruth goes back to the cottage, grabs her jacket from the hook inside the front door, checks to make sure there's a notebook and pencil on the bench outside, in case a customer comes by wanting to order salmon flies when she's off on the milk run. Then she grabs her bicycle from where it leans against the wall of the shed, hurtles aboard the seat and pedals quickly down the lane. Socks streaks along beside her, keeping level with the front wheel.

Mr. Munro isn't in the yard outside the farm like usual, but Ned is there, hitched up to the wagon and ready to go. Ruth palms him a carrot from the pocket of her jumper, where she also has several apples stashed for bribes during the morning route, in case the cart horse decides to be stubborn.

"Good boy," she says, stroking the side of his face while he chomps on the carrot.

There are no milk canisters on the floor of the wagon. Usually, it's fully loaded by the time Ruth arrives at the farm.

"Wait here," she says to Socks. She walks across the dirt in the direction of the barn.

Mr. Munro is nowhere to be seen, but his wife is struggling to manoeuvre one of the metal milk canisters across the swayback floor of the barn. Ruth rushes to help her.

"Let me," she says. "Is your husband ill today?"

"Signed up."

"But he's a farmer."

Farmers are exempt from service because they grow and provide food.

Mrs. Munro straightens up, putting a hand into the small of her back and arching over it. There's a telltale bump visible beneath the front of her apron.

"He wanted to go," she says. "His brothers have all gone. Dan isn't one to be left behind. He's the eldest. It's a matter of principle."

"But you're pregnant."

"Yes. Don't think I'm happy about it."

It's unclear whether she means the pregnancy or her husband's absence during it.

"Stand aside," says Ruth. "You can't be doing this sort of work in your condition." She clamps both arms around the canister and manages to wrestle it over to the wagon, then returns to the barn to perform the same task with the remainder of the milk cans.

Mrs. Munro watches Ruth struggle.

"You're going to be exhausted before you even begin the milk run," she says. "I'll have one of the lads who works the fields come and load the wagon tomorrow morning."

"No. I'm fine." Ruth is leaning against the running board, trying to catch her breath. "It will be good for me. Make me fitter. I'll just get up half an hour earlier. Don't change anything, Mrs. Munro."

"Call me Evelyn."

"Don't change anything, Evelyn. We'll just go on as usual. We can manage."

Ruth vaguely remembers Evelyn from school. They were a year apart. She has a foggy memory of seeing Evelyn in the schoolyard, playing hopscotch with her friends.

Ruth climbs up into the wagon, whistles for Socks, who is digging at the base of a tree near the drive shed, and they lurch out of the farmyard and into the road.

Giles, the milkman, was one of the first men in the village to be called up. When Ruth volunteered to take on some of the work of the absent male villagers, she was offered the choice of the milk run or the postal route. She chose the milk run because she liked the idea of working with the horse. The post is delivered by bicycle.

Ned, the horse, has been with Giles for years, and he has not taken kindly to the switch in handlers. Even with the copious amounts of carrots and apples that Ruth bribes him with every day, there is always at least one moment during the milk run when he stops dead in the road and refuses to budge. It is as if he forgets that Giles is gone, and then suddenly remembers, and in the remembering, he proves his loyalty to his real master by ignoring the wishes of this new, temporary, one.

Today, Ned decides to halt on a lonely stretch of the coast road, in front of a gorse bush. He stamps his feet and sways from side to side, trying to wriggle free from the wagon shafts.

Ruth hops down, carrot in hand, and holds it out to Ned while backing up slowly so that he will have to start walking after her if he wants to reach the carrot.

Ned stares at the carrot, not moving.

"Come on," says Ruth. She waves the carrot in front of his nose. "Please. We're late as it is."

Socks's whole focus on the milk run is the moment when the wagon stops in front of a house and the householder comes out with jugs to be filled from the canisters and, in the transfer from one container to another, milk is spilled on the ground, which the dog then helpfully laps up. Socks doesn't care for Ned, and he especially doesn't like it when Ned stops in the road, nowhere near a house. The collie stands beside Ruth and barks at the horse.

Whether it's the annoying sound of the dog or the lure of the carrot, Ned reluctantly begins to move forward again, but ambles so slowly that Ruth is able to walk alongside him, keeping perfect pace.

When she finally finishes the route, an hour later than she is meant to, she returns to the farm, hands Ned over to one of the farm workers and races home on her bicycle to start work on her salmon fly orders for the day.

The next morning, she leaves her cottage before the sun is up.

Evelyn is waiting for her in the barn.

"I've thought of a solution," she says. She waves her hand towards the bank of milk canisters and Ruth sees, in front of them on the floor, a child's wooden wagon.

"We use one wagon to get to the other wagon," says Evelyn.

"Genius," says Ruth.

Evelyn smiles. "Well, I wouldn't go that far," she says. "But it does solve our problem."

It takes hardly any time to move the milk canisters from the barn to the floorboards of the wagon. Ruth didn't need to get up early after all, as it is still dark when she has finished loading the milk.

"I'm going to make you a cup of tea before you head off," says Evelyn. "You didn't have any breakfast, did you?"

"No," admits Ruth. It was too dark to see properly when she left her cottage. She didn't have time to grope around in the kitchen, looking for something to eat, and it didn't seem worth it to go to the bother of lighting one of the paraffin lamps.

The farmhouse kitchen is cozy and cheerful, much nicer than Ruth's meagre worktop and old cooker. She sits at the big wooden table, watching Evelyn fix a pot of tea, scrape some toast with marmalade.

"You won't go hungry at least," says Evelyn, putting down a plate in front of Ruth, pouring her a cup of tea.

"That's very kind of you."

"Nonsense. It's our milk you're delivering. My milk now, I suppose." Evelyn sits down opposite Ruth. "Dan said it will be over by Christmas."

"The war?"

"What else."

Ruth crunches into her toast, washes it down with a mouthful of hot tea. "I hope so. I don't know how much longer I can do battle with Ned."

"Horses can be very stubborn."

Evelyn sips her tea and Ruth makes a mental note to try to eat and drink more delicately, instead of stuffing food into her mouth like a dog and gulping her liquids. Often, at home, she doesn't even sit down to eat, always in a hurry to get back to work.

"I want Dan to be home for the baby's birth," Evelyn says. "I don't like to think he might still be overseas."

"That was what happened to me," says Ruth. "To my father. He was fighting in France when I was born. He didn't see me until I was three years old."

"I'm sorry about your father, Ruth. Cancer is a nasty business."

"Yes. I mean, thank you. They didn't discover it until it was too late. He just thought he had a backache from clambering about on the river."

"May I ask you something?" Evelyn tops up their cups with tea, doesn't wait for Ruth's reply to her question. "Is that why you wear his clothes? Because he died so recently?"

Ruth rubs the worn fabric of her father's suit jacket.

"I didn't want his clothes to go to waste, I suppose." She pauses. "I should go. It's getting light out now."

Evelyn walks with Ruth outside. The sun is rising over the fields. "I'm sorry," she says. "I didn't mean to upset you. I was just curious."

They stop by the wagon.

"I remember him coming back from France," Ruth says. "I think it's my first real memory, seeing him walking through the front door in his uniform. He picked me up and swung me around. No one had ever done that before. I remember how it felt. Like flying."

Evelyn takes Ruth's hand and puts it on her stomach. They both stand very still, concentrating. The morning sun inches into the farmyard. The baby flutters under Ruth's hand like a salmon in the river.

The war continues past Christmas. Evelyn's baby is born, a girl that she names Ava. Her mother moves in with her to help out. Ruth's mother follows her eldest daughters, who have fled south into marriage.

"They will have families," she says to Ruth, about her decision to leave Brora. "You don't need me here."

Often, in the mornings when Ruth comes to the farm to fetch the horse and wagon, Evelyn is inside with the baby, and Ruth ferries the milk canisters out to the yard by herself.

But one morning, Evelyn is inside the barn when Ruth arrives to get the cans. She waves a postcard under Ruth's nose.

"I wanted to show you this," she says. "It's from Giles, asking after his horse. I don't think he's even written his wife yet."

Ruth takes the postcard, studies it.

"He's a POW," she says. The card has the camp's address in the far-left corner and two words blacked out by the censor in the main body of the text. "Shall we write him back? He might like a letter."

"Tell him all about his horse?"

"In agonizing detail."

After the milk run, Ruth stays on, sitting in Evelyn's kitchen, balancing the baby on her lap, while Evelyn searches out a fresh sheet of paper and a pen. Evelyn's mother is out in the yard, collecting eggs from the coop. Ruth watches her slump across the dirt on her way to the henhouse. She has the same weariness about her as Annie does, a heaviness that Ruth thinks must come not just from the war but from motherhood itself.

"Got it," says Evelyn, coming back into the kitchen. She puts the paper down on the table. "Now, what do we say?"

"Dear Giles."

"After that."

"Ned is a terrible horse. But Ned misses you. Ned only wants to deliver the milk with you. He doesn't care about contributing to the war effort." Ruth bounces Ava on her knee and the baby smiles at her.

"Dear Giles," writes Evelyn. She frowns in concentration. "Why don't we describe the milk run today?"

"Ned stopped outside the bakery," says Ruth. "Then he stopped by the cricket pitch and again out on the drover's road. I fed him so many apples and carrots that he developed a bad case of wind, and I could no longer sit behind him because the stench was so awful, so I had to walk for miles."

"Well, I can't write that." Evelyn is smiling.

"We'll have to make it up then," says Ruth. "Like a fairy tale."

They concoct a story of Ned the wonder horse for Giles in his German prison, and for Ava, who giggles with delight when Ruth wanders off script and imitates the farting horse.

Evelyn's mother returns with her basket of eggs. Ruth leaves on her bicycle with Socks running beside her, licking his lips in a manner that suggests he's been gleefully feasting on the dollops of fresh manure in the yard.

The new gillie is waiting for Ruth when she gets back to her cottage. She's met him a few times before but is still shy around him. It feels odd to her that her father can be replaced so easily, and that no one but her seems to mind, or even notice, the switch. The new gillie is Ruth's age and without a family. He must rattle around inside her old home, leaving many of the rooms unused.

"I meant to write out my order," he says as Ruth disembarks from her bicycle. "But I saw you in the distance, coming up the road." He follows her into her work shed, sits on the chair in the corner without being asked to stay.

"What do you need?"

"Thunder and Lightning. Two perhaps?"

He is polite, knows she is the former gillie's daughter and has respect for her because of this.

"Are you going to wait?"

"If I may."

Ruth wishes he hadn't sat down and that she hadn't given him a choice of staying. She could have told him she is behind on her orders (which is true) and sent him on his way, delivering the flies to him later in the day. It's not as if she doesn't know where to find him. In fact, it might be nice to see the house again. Or it might not. Graham probably doesn't have her mother's flair for making the most from the least.

"Is there going to be a storm?" she asks.

"Not that I'm aware of."

"You do know that this fly works best in stormy weather. It's fairly useless at other times." Ruth can't stop the annoyed tone from creeping into her voice, can't stop the advice. She might begrudge him the job of gillie after all, even though she tells herself that she doesn't.

"I do." Graham shifts his position on the chair. Ruth can hear it creak behind her. "I'm just missing that fly from my wallet. Lost my last one to a salmon two weeks ago. I like to be prepared, to have everything on hand. You never know what to expect."

You should know what to expect. It's your job, thinks Ruth, but thankfully, she doesn't say it out loud.

It's excruciating to have him sitting there waiting for the flies, so Ruth works at her quickest speed, usually reserved for VIPs like HRH. It's a speed that's not sustainable. She can only do a few flies at this velocity before making a mistake.

"There," she says, clipping the last bit of thread and applying a drop of wax to seal it. "Done. You can be on your way."

"It was a real pleasure watching you work." Graham stands up, hands Ruth the money for the flies. "I knew you were good, but I didn't expect you to be that fast." He puts a hand on the doorknob of the shed, opens the door and then turns back to Ruth. "If you would ever like to see your old house, you would be most welcome."

He has good manners. Ruth will grant him that.

"Perhaps," she says, more gruffly than she means. She has already decided against it.

But she does go to see the house. She can't help herself. She's curious about what might have changed, what will have remained the same.

The hens are gone.

"I don't eat many eggs," says Graham. "I've never been partial to them."

Surprisingly, he has kept up her mother's flower garden, and her habit of cutting bouquets to bring inside the house. When Ruth visits, there is a very nice arrangement of rhododendrons on the kitchen table.

The box room is smaller than she remembers and looks even tinier because it is empty.

"I don't really have much," says Graham, who has followed her up the stairs.

"It's a house for a family," says Ruth.

"Well, I still have some hope there." Graham casually puts his arms up inside the door jamb, essentially blocking her exit. She contemplates running at him like a bull, but stands stock still instead, waiting for him to lower his arms, which he does, after an awkward moment. She doesn't like the feeling of being trapped in her old bedroom, so Ruth bolts downstairs and heads outside. Socks is sniffing around the empty chicken coop, looking for traces of the former inhabitants.

"Will you come to the house again?" asks Graham.

"I don't think so."

"May I come and visit you then?" His face is red and he looks embarrassed. Ruth softens. She has been a little too hard on him.

"Come in an evening," she says. "I stop work at sundown."

But it is Evelyn who shows up on an evening. A Friday evening, when Ruth is sitting in the garden, enjoying the sound of the distant sea and the fragrance of the flowers that twine beneath her kitchen window. It is the first warm day in ages, the first time she has been able to sit out.

"Hello," Evelyn says, suddenly appearing at the top of the lane and startling Ruth.

"Hello."

"So, this is your lair." Evelyn unlatches the gate and comes across the garden. She is wearing a dress without an apron and has her hair up.

"It's beautiful," says Evelyn, staring out at the sea, which is laid like a blue tablecloth across the horizon.

"I look at it all day," says Ruth, "so it's hard to think about it being anything. But I would miss it if it wasn't there." She is thrown by Evelyn's presence in her garden. "You don't have the baby with you?"

"My mother is looking after her. I'm on my way to the dance."

"But the dance is the other direction."

The hall where the ceilidhs are held is at the edge of the village, not this way up the coast road.

"I've come to petition you," says Evelyn. "We're down men because of the war, and since you have the kit and look the part, I've come to ask if you'd help us out."

"I don't dance," says Ruth.

"Don't, as in you've never learned, or don't, as in you're just not interested?"

The whisper of the surf sounds like a voice, murmuring just beyond the road. It brings back, unbidden, the lines from a poem that Ruth once had to memorize in school. *Begin, and cease, and then again begin, / With tremulous cadence slow, and bring / The eternal note of sadness in.*

"I never learned. It wasn't something my parents ever did, or encouraged us to do. They moved here, but essentially, they remained British. Dancing wasn't for them."

"Would you be willing?" Evelyn reaches down, extending her hand to Ruth. "To give it a go?"

It's the chivalrous gesture more than the idea of dancing that moves Ruth.

"Yes," she says, taking Evelyn's outstretched hand. "I'd be willing."

Highlander

THE VILLAGE HALL IS PACKED, OVERFULL, with people spilling across the steps and down onto the lawn around the building. Ruth, used to evenings with the dim, smoky light from her paraffin lamps, is blinded by the brightness of the interior and has to put her hand over her eyes when they enter the building.

Evelyn misreads the gesture, thinks instead that Ruth is overwhelmed by the sheer number of people inside the hall.

"Don't worry," she says, taking Ruth by the arm and leading her away from the dancers in the middle of the floor. "We'll just stand over here for a bit so you can get used to it."

They lean against the wall, just inside the door. At the opposite end of the hall, the band energetically launches into a jig, then a reel. Evelyn is tapping her hand against her knee, her foot against the floor.

"Go and dance," says Ruth, nudging her. "I'll watch you. Learn a thing or two that way."

It's all about patterns, Ruth can see that after a while. There's the pattern of the music, swinging out and in, repeating, and there's the pattern of the dance that mimics the tune somewhat but also creates its own design on the wooden floor. The music moves in a circle. The dancers move in a circle. She watches Evelyn twirl with her partner, an old man Ruth recognizes from the fishmonger's.

After a couple of dances, Evelyn comes back, her face flushed.

"What do you think?" she asks. "Ready to give it a try?"

"I wouldn't want to let you down," says Ruth. "You're very good. I'd be beginner clumsy, get in your way. Tread on your toes."

Evelyn takes Ruth's hand, for the second time that evening, a fact that Ruth registers very clearly.

"Come on," she says, tugging Ruth towards the door. "I've got an idea."

They walk outside, around to the back of the hall, where they can hear the music clearly through the walls. The moon makes the grass look like a dark lake, like the waters of Loch Brora when Ruth was there once with her father at night. He was looking for a rod and reel a client had accidentally left on the shore. She remembers the blackness of the water, its shiny surface, how, at one point, her father got on his hands and knees to feel around for the fishing rod. He eventually found it by tripping over it.

Evelyn hooks her elbow in Ruth's, spins her slowly around on the lawn.

"This is a spin," she says. "We can spin right, or left."

They hook opposite elbows and spin the other way.

The moon goes behind a cloud and there's just the glow from the windows of the hall to see by.

Evelyn gives instruction and they spin and dance down an imaginary line, spin again. Ruth remembers the patterns from inside the hall, plays them over in her mind as she searches out Evelyn's hand, the crook of her elbow.

"You're a natural," says Evelyn.

"I'm just a quick learner," says Ruth.

The music changes and they start again, this time not talking, no instruction needed.

Ruth goes to the dances every week after that.

If there's not a ceilidh in Brora, then she drives over to neighbouring villages and takes part there. Sometimes, Evelyn comes with her, but often, she has to remain at home because of Ava or the farm, or because she has given her mother a much needed night off instead.

Ruth is fine on her own. She is good, in fact, at being alone, and her confidence with dancing grows each time she steps out onto the floor, but she always prefers the Friday or Saturday nights when Evelyn can slip the lead of family and farm life and accompany her.

It is best when they are dancing, no talking, the music a current that moves them this way and that. The mass of people in the hall, spinning and stepping, turning together, is not unlike the way salmon move as one in the rivers, and Ruth likes to think about this as she is skipping over the floor, carried along by the beat of a tune.

All week now she waits for the night of dancing, sitting in her tin shed, fastening feathers and wool to steel hooks, watching the rain bead on the window and humming the tune to a waltz.

Graham comes to visit her. He likes to tell her stories about his clients, and the fish that have been caught on the flies that Ruth has made. He sits on the chair in the corner of her shed, drinking tea from his flask, while hers goes cold in front of her on the work table, because she can't make herself stop tying to drink it.

"You'll never guess what happened this week," Graham says.

Ruth waits for him to continue, winding on a layer of silver thread.

"Are you guessing?"

"Do you really want me to?"

"Yes."

"You were eaten by a salmon."

"Close."

Ruth turns around in her chair. "How can that be close?" she says. "You're sitting in my shed, not a mark on you."

Graham reaches into the pocket of his jacket, pulls out his fly wallet. He opens it and holds it up for Ruth to see, pointing to a fly in the upper right corner of the wallet.

"The Duke caught a twelve pounder at Stoney Pools with one of your Highlanders. This one. And when we hauled the fish out and I'd given it last rites, we found another of your Highlanders hanging from its mouth. An older one. This one." He points to a fly directly below the first one. "Someone fishing in the same conditions, with the same fly, but maybe years previous."

"Months perhaps," says Ruth. "It was only a twelve pounder."

But she is impressed—not with Graham for telling her the story, or the Duke for catching the twice-hooked fish, but with the salmon itself, who clearly had preferred the Highlander above other flies, and who had died because of this preference.

"The fish had good taste," she says. "I like that fly myself."

Saturday night, Ruth takes extra time to get ready. It promises to be a special evening. She is to pick Evelyn up in her car and they are driving south to Dornoch for a ceilidh in the castle there. She chooses a relatively clean white shirt, a silk tie with ducks on it, overtop of her usual tweed skirt. Her leather shoes are scuffed and dirty.

"They need some spit and polish," she says to Socks, fetching the shoe cleaning rag and paste from the cupboard under the sink.

Evelyn is waiting on the front stoop when Ruth slams on the brakes in the farmyard, sending up a cloud of dust.

"Sorry," she says, leaping out to open the passenger door for Evelyn. "I took the turn too fast up the drive."

Evelyn brushes her hands across the front of

her dress before getting into the car. "No one could accuse you of being dull," she says.

The seaside hotel in Dornoch has recently been requisitioned by the army, so the owners of the castle have offered up their home for the ceilidh. There are candles as big as pillars burning inside the front door, suits of armour standing at attention in the great hall.

Ruth peers through the visor of one of the helmets.

"Hot work being a knight," she says. "And you wouldn't be able to see a bloody thing from inside there."

"Good to be protected by armour then," says Evelyn.

The great hall has a fireplace at either end, each one big enough for an entire family to stand inside it. The ceiling beams are blackened with age. Ruth puts her hand up and traces the indentation of an axe strike on the wood just above her head.

"Don't skip too vigorously," she says to Evelyn. "Or you'll conk yourself one."

With the low ceilings and the two fires burning with gusto in the great hall, dancing is sweaty and exhausting. Evelyn pulls Ruth out of the fray after a reel and a jig.

"Come on," she says. "Let's go exploring."

The hallways are labyrinthine and barely lit, hung with threadbare tapestries and portraits. They hold hands so as not to lose each other in the gloom.

"It's as bad as my cottage at night," says Ruth, which makes Evelyn laugh, because, of course, the darkness of the hallways is the only thing that Ruth's modest cottage and the grand castle have in common.

The hallways are abandoned in favour of the staircase, wide at the bottom like the skirt of a ball gown, tapering up to a waist of a landing.

"Let's find the tower," says Evelyn, pulling Ruth behind her up the next flight of stairs.

The tower room is through a heavy oak door studded with iron. The door swings open into the room, which is empty except for a four-poster bed. There's no fire in the grate, no sign of habitation. There are no linens on the bed. They leave the door open to borrow a little of the light that funnels up the staircase and trickles into the tower.

"Do you think this was where they put the prisoners once?" asks Ruth, going over to the window and peering through the mullioned panes. She can see the distant lights of the village houses, winking like stars in the darkness. She feels impossibly tall.

"Yes."

"They had a good view."

"It wouldn't have helped them any."

Evelyn comes and stands beside Ruth and they peer down through the window together.

"Terrible to be locked up," Evelyn says. "To be confined to one room for your whole life."

Ruth thinks of her work shed, of the hours and hours she spends there, staring out to sea, making her lures from bright bits of feathers and coloured wool, the miles and miles of thread she winds in a single year.

"I think I might be a prisoner," she says.

"No. Not you." Evelyn puts a hand up to Ruth's face. "You're the freest person I know." She leans in and kisses Ruth lightly on the cheek.

Back in the great hall, they are in time for refreshments—glasses of sherry and little sandwiches without the crusts, handed round by the owners of the castle themselves. Ruth holds her glass up to the fire to watch the light refract through the crystal.

"It would be all pomp and ceremony," she says to Evelyn. "If you lived in a castle. Do you think you would have to change for each meal?"

"Perhaps not for breakfast," says Evelyn.

"Could I come down in my dressing gown?"

"To a sideboard groaning with covered silver dishes. And a butler to serve you."

"Bacon and eggs? Fried bread? My usual grilled tomato?"

"And kippers," says Evelyn.

"Please, no fish." Ruth is decisive.

The music starts up again and the next dance is to be Machine without Horses.

"Let's have a go at this one," says Ruth. "It's my absolute favourite."

Afterwards, they walk across the lawn to the car, the grass springy underfoot and the scent of rosemary wafting through the air from a giant clay urn on the terrace.

"Everything's oversize at the castle," says Ruth. She opens the car door for Evelyn. "Milady," she says, and Evelyn giggles.

The road is empty. The moon polishes the fields to a shine on either side of them. When Ruth takes a corner too quickly, Evelyn falls against her and stays there, her head resting on Ruth's shoulder.

"It's lovely where we live, isn't it," Evelyn says.

"My father used to say there was no more perfect place on earth."

"And what do you say?"

"That there's no more perfect place on earth."

Ruth slows the car when she enters the driveway to the farm, but arrival is impossible to prevent.

They inch up into the yard.

"That's funny," says Evelyn. "All the lights are on." She still has her head resting on Ruth's shoulder, even after Ruth has brought the car to a standstill.

The windows are ablaze in Evelyn's farmhouse, and the curtains aren't pulled in the front room. Ruth watches as a man leans against the glass, peers out at her car in the yard.

Evelyn jerks upright. "Oh Lord, that's Dan," she says. "He's home."

With Dan returned from the war, Ruth doesn't see Evelyn in the mornings anymore when she comes to fetch the horse and cart. There is no shunting the milk canisters from the barn on the child's wagon. Now, the cans are already loaded on the cart when Ruth rides up on her bicycle. When she returns, at the end of the milk run, one of the field hands takes Ned from her. Sometimes she sees Evelyn watching her from the window of the front room. Ruth waves, but Evelyn has only once waved back.

At the dances, Ruth has other partners now. Evelyn doesn't show.

"Her husband's back," says Harriet, the butcher's wife. "She can't be gallivanting about anymore."

Still, Ruth waits for Evelyn's return, looks hopefully towards the sound of the doors creaking open at the village hall, or the latch of her cottage gate lifting with a squeak in the rain.

And finally, one morning, when Ruth is just climbing up onto the loaded cart at the farm, Evelyn rushes from the house towards her.

"I'm sorry," she says, grabbing onto Ruth's arm with both of her hands. "Dan has had great need of me these past weeks. And he's sent my mother home, so I always have Ava now."

"It must be good to have him back again. I'm happy for you." Ruth reaches into the breast pocket of her jacket. "I've been carrying this around for ages. I made it weeks ago." She passes the salmon fly to Evelyn. "It's a Highlander. To remind you of the dancing. And the castle." She shifts from one foot to the other. "And to remind you of me."

Evelyn looks down at the lure in her palm. "It's beautiful," she says. There are tears in her eyes as she slowly closes her hand around the fly.

Wilkinson

Ruth goes for a proper date with Graham, on a picnic to the scenic Glen of the Fairies. She drives them because Graham doesn't have a car. He seems unused to being driven, clutching the strap that hangs down from the roof and making phantom braking motions with his feet whenever Ruth goes hard round a bend.

"You took that last one rather fast," he says as Ruth grimly speeds up. She usually enjoys driving, but there is no joy in it today and she just wants to get there as quickly as possible to escape Graham's nervous twitches and constant cautions.

It's better when they are out of the car, walking over the uneven ground, the hills rising softly before them. Graham carries the picnic basket and blanket, and Socks runs ahead after a pheasant. Ruth unclenches her hands, stretches her fingers to feel the wind spool between them.

"Would this be a good spot, do you think?" Graham has stopped in front of a grassy hollow surrounded by a semicircle of large stones.

"It looks nice." Ruth watches as Graham unrolls the blanket and weights the corners down with rocks. She opens the picnic hamper and takes out the plates and cutlery, the potted meat sandwiches and bottles of beer.

"Delicious," says Graham, already biting into one of the sandwiches.

"Glad you like them." Ruth didn't actually make the sandwiches. She's not much of a cook and it made her nervous to think of what she might get wrong in even something so simple as the assembly of a sandwich. Her friend Millie made the food.

"You'll have to learn to cook properly if you're to marry him," said Millie, but she did Ruth's bidding and prepared the picnic for her.

Ruth nibbles around the edge of her sandwich. When she was a child, she would have pretended to be a mouse. Now she has to pretend to be interested in Graham.

Socks returns with muddy paws and plops himself down in the middle of the blanket.

"Off!" says Graham, kicking at the dog with his boot. Socks inches back towards Ruth and she puts a hand on his head and scratches him through his thick fur. It is clear that Graham has never had a dog, or he wouldn't be so irritated by Socks.

The beer makes everything more tolerable. Ruth has to make an effort not to down her bottle in one swallow, and then has to make an effort not to belch.

The sun comes out from behind the clouds and they take off their shoes, lean back against the stones after they have eaten. Ruth thinks that Graham might try to hold her hand, but he doesn't. He closes his eyes and dozes. Socks has wandered off again. Ruth watches a line of ants ferry a bread-crumb from the blanket to a small hole near the rocks. She pokes at the ground with a twig and flexes her toes inside her stockings.

When the rain starts, they wait for it to pass, and when it doesn't, they stuff the picnic gear back into the basket, grab the blanket and hightail it for the car. There's a moment of laughter as they cram everything into the boot, but then Socks comes hurling towards them and Ruth lets him into the back seat.

"That dog stinks," says Graham when they are all in the car and Ruth has started the engine.

Ruth unwinds her window a little, in an attempt to staunch the potent smell of wet dog, but it doesn't do much good.

Graham suddenly launches himself at Ruth over the gearshift, pinning her against her door, his lips cold and wet from the rain, his tongue muscling into her open mouth. She fights back, then realizes that he is kissing her and tries to relax. After a few moments, he pulls himself off her and settles back into his seat, and she puts the stick into reverse and backs out of the parking space.

The rain continues. The road darkens with it, and the sky seals shut with clouds.

"There will be good fishing tomorrow," says Graham. "If this keeps up. I have two gents from London, up for the week."

"Are they staying with you?" Graham often rents out the empty rooms in his cottage to visiting fishermen, as a way to make a little extra money.

"No. At the hotel. You should join us there for a drink one evening. They've heard of you, asked if I knew you."

It seems extraordinary to Ruth that her slow production, one fly at a time, has resulted in gaining her a reputation among salmon fishers, has granted her a small measure of fame.

"Come in for a cup of tea," says Graham when they get to his cottage, and Ruth does because she can't think of a polite way to refuse.

While the kettle is boiling, she goes upstairs to use the loo, the indoor water closet a recent addition to the cottage. When she lived there with her parents and sisters, they used an old earth closet behind the house, which had a door that was too short. The snow blew under it in the winter and burned her legs.

She pulls the chain, watches the water sluice lazily around the toilet bowl. On the window ledge is a mug of shaving soap and a razor. Ruth picks up the razor and examines the tiny hairs along the blade. Graham's face hadn't felt that smooth when he'd pressed it against her in the car. The razor and its wedge-shaped blade is a Wilkinson, which is the same name as one of the salmon flies she ties. One bears no resemblance to the other.

Downstairs, Graham has made the tea and it's stewing under its knitted cozy on the kitchen table. He's put out a plate of digestives beside it, the good kind, with one side covered in milk chocolate.

"Meet with your approval?" he asks, but Ruth isn't sure if he means the spread or the cottage or the new upstairs loo, so she doesn't reply.

The rain lashes against the windows. Graham didn't want Socks in the house and Ruth hopes that he's found Shep's old doghouse and is sheltering there. She should have just left him in the back seat of the car, but he is hard to keep contained if he thinks there is exploring to be done.

"It could do with a woman's touch," says Graham.

"What could?"

"This cottage."

"It had a woman's touch until quite recently," says Ruth. It's only been a few years since her mother went down south to be with Eliza and Marjory, and her handiwork in the gillie's cottage is still very much in evidence.

Graham reaches across the table and grasps Ruth's hand in his own. His hand is strong and his skin feels coarse, not unlike the way her father's hand felt when she held it on their way down to the river when she was a little girl.

"Ruth," he says, "I'm trying. Go easy on me."

His hand shakes with nerves. Ruth pulls away, cruelly.

Socks is waiting out the rain under the overhang of the old henhouse, although he is still wet through, shakes all over Ruth when they get back into the car. When they arrive home, she banks a fire in the grate, rubs Socks down with an old bit of towelling.

She spreads the picnic blanket on the floor in front of the fireplace and eats what's left of the food straight out of the basket, Socks curled up against her outstretched legs, the sound of the rain hitting the windows almost like music behind them.

Mar Lodge

RUTH EXCHANGES HER MILK ROUTE FOR THE volunteer job of being a coastwatcher. It pains her to go to Evelyn's farm and not see Evelyn, and now that there's talk of a German invasion, more people are needed to guard the Scottish shoreline. Barbed wire has been placed on all the beaches and there are huts on stilts along the coast so that volunteers can train their spyglasses on the sky and sea, in the hopes of spotting enemy ships or aircraft before they get too close.

With the new job, Ruth gets a uniform and a motorbike, both of which please her. She likes the smart cut of the jacket and the shiny buttons, the jaunty angle of the hat, and she especially likes the khaki green motorbike, complete with sidecar. Petrol rations have made driving her car difficult, and she only uses it now once or twice a week, so she is grateful to be able to have the motorbike instead, burning the army's petrol rather than her own.

She learns to operate the motorbike in a class with other women who are training to be coast wardens. The smaller girls have trouble with the kick-start on the BSA, but Ruth is not timid, stomps on it for all she's worth and never misses firing up the engine. She is also very good at navigating around the pylons that have been set up at the edge of the airfield in Dornoch. She is the first to pass the test and roars off on the bike while the others are still wobbling around the course.

"You can always go faster than you think," the training sergeant said to her, and Ruth takes him at his word, rolling on the throttle around every bend in the road.

As a warden, she reports on the activity in the huts along her section of coast, compiling the reports from a dozen different huts and passing them along to her commanding officer, the British Captain Asher. She also takes a few shifts a week at the coastal hut just up the road from her cottage, which strikes her as a bit ridiculous, as she has a perfectly good view of the sea from her shed and could just as soon watch from there and not miss out on three afternoons of tying flies. She is as busy as ever in that capacity. The war has halted or curtailed many things, but fishing hasn't been one of them.

The hut is very basic, a simple square, wooden structure. Inside, it has a single chair, a ledge along the window side that holds the logbook and spyglasses, and Ruth's lunch, when she remembers to bring it. Socks isn't allowed into the hut, but he lies right outside the door. On the days that start with rain, Ruth leaves him at home.

Her system while in the hut is to scan the sea from left to right, and then scan the sky from right to left, moving the spyglasses incrementally across the horizon, each scan taking about two minutes. Then she lets five minutes lapse before repeating, timing this break with the old watch of her father's that she has worn on her wrist since the day he died. During the five-minute break, she goes outside, if the weather is good, and throws a stick for Socks or walks round and round the hut for a bit of exercise. When it is rainy, she works out fly patterns on a bit of paper inside the hut. Now that she is so expert at tying the traditional patterns, she is trying to invent some new patterns of her own.

At week's end, she drives the motorbike down to Dornoch, with Socks in the sidecar, a fact that thrills the children of Brora, who chase after the bike when she roars through the village. Socks even wears his own pair of goggles, which he tolerates without complaint. When Ruth corners too fast, he puts a paw against the lip of the sidecar to steady himself. He appears to enjoy the motorbike as much as Ruth does.

Captain Asher always has a bit of biscuit in his pocket for Socks.

"There you go, Sergeant Socks," he says, handing over the better part of a digestive. "And you, Private Thomas, come inside and I'll make us a cup of tea."

It is their joke that Captain Asher ranks the dog above Ruth, but it makes her smile every time. She follows him into the hotel, which looks remarkably unchanged, except for the fact that there are soldiers sleeping in all the guest rooms, and the lounge at the front has become an operations centre, complete with maps and radios. But the front desk still has the hotel register open on the counter, and the room keys hang on the wall behind the desk, just as when Ruth used to sometimes come to deliver flies to one of the guests. When Captain Asher leads her into the breakfast room, there are still stacks of menu cards on the window ledge, flower vases on all the tables.

Captain Asher pulls out the chair for Ruth and then goes off to fetch the tea. Their table is by the window and looks out to the sea, now trussed up in wire.

"It's a shame, isn't it?" Captain Asher is back with two mugs of tea. He places them on the table. "I used to like to go swimming in the mornings, but it's difficult to get onto the beach now."

"It must have been very cold." Ruth has never been swimming in the North Sea. She has been into the loch on several very hot summer days, but even that water is freezing.

"Invigorating." Captain Asher smiles. "It's a novelty to be by the sea. I grew up inland, in Surrey."

"Oh," says Ruth, "I'm from Surrey as well."

"Whereabouts?"

"Walton-on-the-Hill."

"I'm just up the road in Claygate," says Captain Asher. "What do you miss about Surrey?"

"I left when I was just three," says Ruth. She pauses, takes a sip of her tea. "What should I miss?"

"The trees. Most definitely the trees. Oaks that are hundreds of years old. The Beeches." Captain Asher runs a hand through his hair. "All the woodland. It's very beautiful here, but there are no trees."

Ruth has a memory of the window in her bedroom in Walton-on-the-Hill and the oak tree that was outside it, how the birds settled on its branches, how the leaves rustled in the wind.

"I'm so used to the lack of trees that I never think about it," she says. "But now that I am thinking about it, I do remember the oak in our garden."

They drink their tea. Ruth hands over the weekly record logs to Captain Asher. He walks her back outside to her motorbike. Socks is lounging on the grass of the front lawn in the sun, sound asleep.

"I have Sunday off," says Captain Asher as Ruth is climbing aboard the bike. "Would you take me fishing?"

They go to the loch, as Ruth is nervous about meeting up with Graham on the lower reaches of the Brora. Captain Asher hires a boat and they row out to the centre of the lake, and then ship the oars and drift while the captain zigs his line across the water.

"I hope you don't catch a fish," says Ruth. "I wouldn't want to watch you kill it."

"And yet you make the most exquisite lures to do exactly that," says Captain Asher.

"I don't do it to kill the fish."

"But they do get killed nonetheless."

Ruth shifts in the boat, wishing now that she'd never come, or that she'd brought the dog with her for comfort.

"I like the patterns," she says. "I like to help the fishermen. And I'm good at it."

"All perfectly sound reasons. Here, hold this for a moment." Captain Asher passes his rod to Ruth so that he can fix his pipe and light it. "Besides, what's life without a little mystery?"

"You think I'm mysterious?"

"Very. I don't call you Private Thomas for nothing."

Ruth smiles, in spite of herself. "You could call me Ruth," she says, after a while.

"And you can call me John," Captain Asher says, drawing on his pipe, the sweet woodsy smell filling the air between them.

It is surprisingly nice to drift in the boat, even with the alarming prospect of a fish being caught on Captain Asher's line. Ruth trails her hand in the water and watches the clouds scud by, no two ever the same.

There are a few other boats out on the loch, but they all keep apart from each other, keep to their own patch of water. Ruth can see the fishing lines arcing out, the flash of the lures before they hit the surface of the lake. From this distance, the movement looks like a kind of dance. She plays a game with herself, trying to guess what the fly on the end of the line might be, given the conditions of the day. Mar Lodge would be the best choice of salmon fly today, she thinks.

Captain Asher does catch a fish, but he takes it swiftly off the hook and lets it go. Ruth leans over the edge of the boat to watch it shimmy away through the dark water.

"Let me take you to tea," he says after they have been drifting on the loch for the better part of the afternoon.

"I've left my dog," says Ruth. "I can't be out much longer." She pauses. "I could make you tea at my cottage, if you like. But it won't be anything fancy."

"I'm very fond of not fancy," says John, lifting the oars from their resting place on the gunnels of the boat and beginning to row them back to shore.

Ruth makes them beans on toast and they eat at her little table in the parlour, the one she only sits at when she has company. She is nervous to have Captain Asher in her cottage, nervous that he will find it squalid next to the faded luxury of the Dornoch hotel.

"Very cozy," he says when he comes through the front door. "You must be snug here in the winters."

He sits at Ruth's table in the parlour, next to the wireless, and he eats his beans on toast with great speed and enthusiasm. Ruth makes him a second plate, pours them each a glass of sherry. She had meant to serve this before the beans on toast, but she had forgotten her manners. It is easy, when living alone, to neglect the social graces.

"Have you always lived by yourself?" asks Captain Asher. (Ruth has trouble thinking of him as John.)

"Yes. I like it this way."

"How do you know if you've never tried it any other way?"

"Well . . ." Ruth can't think of an answer. "Do you live alone?"

Captain Asher laughs. "Don't think you're getting off that particular hook," he says, pushing his empty plate away. "But yes, I live alone. For now. I have a girl waiting for me down south. It's a good investment to go into war with a girl waiting for you."

Ruth thinks of her father and how he was in France while her mother was pregnant with her, how perhaps the thought of the baby kept him going, the desire to see the baby. Perhaps it was this way for Evelyn's husband as well, that he made sure to keep himself as safe as possible so he could get home and see his child.

"What's her name?" she asks.

"Sarah."

"Will you marry her?"

"I will. Assuming we all get out of this alive."

Captain Asher downs his sherry, holds out his glass for a refill.

"Now," he says, "how do you know that you wouldn't like to live with someone?"

Ruth pours the sherry. Her hand is shaking a little.

"This is what I've always done," she says. "I wouldn't know how to do it differently."

"You're what, twenty-four?"

"Twenty-five."

"'Always' hasn't been very long then." Captain Asher downs his second glass as well. Ruth pours him a third. "Who would you have been, I wonder, if you had remained in Walton-on-the-Hill? The landscape here has given you an identity, given you a profession, but who would you be without that?"

After he has drunk his third glass of sherry and left, Ruth sits at the table in the parlour and thinks about that question for a moment or two. But then there are the dishes to wash and there's still enough light in the sky to go out to the shed and work on her back orders. She crosses the strip of lawn between the cottage and the shed. The light through the clouds is orange, makes the garden glow as though it's lit from within, like a lantern. The flowers look pretty. The grass feels soft underfoot. The stool where she sits to tie flies is comfortable, moulded into the shape of her body. The sea, even with its twist of wire across the beach, is soothing. Ruth secures a treble hook in the vise and gets down to work.

Snow Fly

THE WAR ENDS. THE BARBED WIRE IS unwrapped from Scotland's coastline. Dornoch reclaims its seaside hotel. Ruth buys her now decommissioned motorbike from the British Army, and the coastwatching huts are abandoned to the needs of walkers and lovers.

Captain John Asher returns south and posts Ruth a package a month after he gets home. When she opens it, she finds a handful of acorns and a photograph of him in uniform. She plants the acorns in a row at the bottom of her garden, and she tucks the photograph into the back pages of her fly-tying handbook, the one she thinks of as her "bible."

She misses her wartime jobs more than she thought she would, and for a few weeks, she aimlessly rides her motorbike up and down the coast road, past the string of empty wooden huts, then down to Dornoch, stopping briefly outside the hotel and the deserted airfield before turning for home again.

But business is brisk, and after the war, there are more fishermen from overseas, from Canada and America, coming to try their luck in the Scottish salmon rivers. Ruth, always eager to help the fishermen who just show up at her door, is now getting seriously behind on her orders that arrive through the post. She works with a stack of envelopes on the bench beside her desk, the pile getting higher with each passing day.

She still dances on Friday or Saturday nights and sometimes goes down to Inverness to compete with other dancers from the area. But what she mostly does is work.

First thing in the morning, Ruth lets Socks out. Then she sees to her ablutions. She goes to bed each night with a hot water bottle, and in the morning, she uses the now cold water inside the rubber sleeve to brush her teeth and wash her face. Then she makes herself a real breakfast—eggs, toast, bacon and a grilled tomato. She washes this down with a potful of tea.

By this time, Socks has returned and she puts

his breakfast down for him, usually scraps from last night's dinner mixed with an egg.

After breakfast, she walks across the lawn to the shed. If it is anything other than summer, she turns on the Calor gas heater when she gets inside, to warm the place up a little. Then she settles herself on her stool and Socks lies down on the floor, and she begins tying flies.

The sun is just up at this point. Often, Ruth has her breakfast while it is still dark out, wanting to maximize the daylight hours while she is at work. She sits in front of her vise, which is in front of the window, and she looks out over the North Sea while she winds thread and feathers, bits of coloured wool, onto the different sized hooks. If there are no orders on the bench outside her door from local fishermen, she begins working through the orders that have arrived by post, taking an envelope off the top of the pile, then another, and another. The pile is so big at this point that by the end of the day, even if she has been working solidly through the envelopes, it looks no different from when she began.

Often, Ruth continues right through lunch. This is why she has a proper breakfast before she begins, to last her through the day. There is a rhythm to her work that is hard to interrupt. She ties flies. She looks out the window, still scanning the horizon from habit, then dropping her gaze back to the hook and the vise, the desktop strewn with skins and feathers and bobbins of thread.

At some point in the afternoon, Socks will whine or pace the floor of the shed, asking to be let out. Ruth will take him for a walk through the fields behind her cottage, and when they return, she will make herself a cup of tea and give Socks his dinner. She will take her tea back to the shed, putting a saucer on top of it to keep it hot while she returns to work, and then drink the tea when it is cold, much later on, after she has forgotten about it.

In the summer, it is light until almost midnight, and Ruth can extend her working day right up until the edge of civil twilight, when the dark blue of the sky is ceding to black. In winter, she can only tie flies up until four o'clock, as the winter dark comes so soon.

Twice a week, she gets in her car and goes to town. She brings with her a multitude of empty containers to fill with water from the hotel bar, where she has a friend who works there most afternoons. Ruth also goes to the post office, to send out the salmon flies she has made, and she visits the grocer and butcher and baker to replenish her rations for the week.

Some of the people who order her flies by sending a letter include the fee inside the envelope. Other fishermen, she has to bill. Ruth has no rule for how she wants to receive and process orders and just deals with what comes her way. If there is money included in an envelope with a salmon fly order, excellent. If she has to bill a client, that is also fine. She never established rules at the beginning, so it seems impossible to impose them now.

On the days when Ruth goes to the village, she drives past Evelyn's farm and always looks out the car window at the farmyard, hoping for a glimpse of Evelyn, but has never seen her. Once, she watched Dan leading a horse across the yard, and she saw a young girl, who must have been Ava, running towards the house. But mostly, Ruth drives by and just sees the muddy flat of the yard, the barn and the stone farmhouse, all without anybody nearby.

Back home again, Ruth will unload her containers of water, carry them into her kitchen and stow them under the sink. She will take her groceries from her shopping basket and store them in the larder. If it is summer, she will go back out to the shed and set to work again. If it is winter, she will make herself supper—always something simple like beans on toast or a boiled egg, maybe a sausage roll she bought from the bakery. In summer, she will eat late, and will still be able to go out to the shed for a couple of hours afterwards. In winter, she eats early and then settles down to listen to the wireless for the evening, or, if she feels energetic, do one of the DIY jobs that she has written down on the master list she keeps on the table beside the wireless. She likes to wallpaper and has been slowly working her way through the rooms and hallways of her cottage, covering all of them in different patterns of wallpaper. She is partial to narrative scenes with animals or birds in them.

Ruth has no telephone. She has no electricity. She does have running water, but she feels that the source of the water is too near to a sheep pasture and that it is contaminated with waste from the sheep, so she prefers to use water from the village that she collects in jugs. She goes dancing every week. Very rarely, she has supper out at the hotel with a client or friend. She is not much of a drinker and while she enjoys a glass of sherry and, occasionally, a whisky, she never drinks alone. She doesn't smoke cigarettes, although she likes the smell of pipe tobacco. She seldom drops in on anyone, but she is constantly being visited by fishermen who need salmon flies or who want to regale her with stories about the fish they have caught using her flies.

At night, in summer, Ruth falls into bed at midnight, sleeping fitfully and waking again to resume work at dawn. In winter, she goes to bed around nine o'clock and sleeps right through until seven the next morning. She never uses an alarm clock, but sleeps with the curtains parted so that she will be awakened by the morning sun slanting in the window. When she lies in bed at night, she listens to the distant hush of the sea falling on the shore. If she dreams, they are mostly panic dreams about not getting through her orders quickly enough. If she is very anxious, she will dream about being chased, or of Socks going missing and not being able to find him. Once, she dreamt about walking with her father into the River Brora, standing in the water and feeling the cold current twine around her legs.

These are the days and nights of Ruth Thomas, aged thirty-two, and she moves through them easily, bending a little this way or that to accommodate a change in plans, or bad weather, or a favour needed from a friend. Mostly, though, one day resembles another, so it is startling when one of the days suddenly becomes markedly different.

It is a winter Tuesday in early December. Ruth has finished work for the day and is in her kitchen boiling a pair of eggs for her supper. Rain is dashing against the windows and walls of the cottage, and there is the noise of water bubbling in its pot on the stove, but Ruth still hears the squeak of the latch lifting on her garden gate. This is followed by a knock at her front door.

It's Evelyn standing on the wooden stoop, soaked through from the rain, her wet hair plastered to the sides of her face. When she steps into Ruth's front hall, water immediately gathers in a puddle on the floor beneath her.

"You're not even wearing a coat," says Ruth, closing the door behind her.

"Dan's father died."

"I'm sorry."

"He was a crusty old sod," says Evelyn. "I mostly tried to avoid him. He wasn't nice like your father."

She leans on Ruth's shoulder and kicks off her shoes.

"I sent Dan down to be with his mother in Aboyne. Ava's gone with him. I said I'd stay behind to do the milking."

"When do you have to do the milking?"

"In the morning."

Evelyn's hand is cold on Ruth's shoulder, but even so, it makes her skin burn.

Ruth turns off her pot of eggs on the stove and uses the water to fill a hot water bottle. She gives Evelyn her dressing gown and hangs Evelyn's wet clothes over the backs of two chairs near the fire in the parlour.

"I'm awfully tired," says Evelyn. "It was such a long way to get to you. It seems as though I've been waiting years."

"It has been years." And yet the ease between them makes it feel as though no time has passed at all. It is, Ruth realizes, because she has always been thinking of Evelyn, even though they have been estranged.

She pours them each a glass of sherry and leads Evelyn down the hallway to her bedroom. "It gets smoky if I light the paraffin lamp in here," she says. "Seeing that it's a small room."

"I don't mind the darkness."

There is not much light from the window because of the rain and the clouds. Ruth knows her way instinctively across the room, but Evelyn has to feel along the wall, so as not to bang into anything.

"You have wallpaper," she says.

"I just finished putting it in this room."

They reach the bed at the same time. It's a twin bed, narrow and soft, but there is room for both of them, and they sit up against the headboard, sipping their glasses of sherry.

"What's on the wallpaper?" asks Evelyn.

"It's pink and white," says Ruth. "The background is white and there are four repeating scenes in pink. There's a headless church, a fancy stone wall with an urn on top of it, a ruined house, and a war memorial. But each of the objects is covered in flowers and trees."

"An abandoned estate," says Evelyn. "But why is there a war memorial? Are you sure it's a war memorial?"

"It's tall and pointed and sits on a patch of grass," says Ruth. "It looks like a war memorial."

"Yes, but the estate sounds older than the first war." Evelyn finds Ruth's hand in the darkness and squeezes it. "I think it's the steeple," she says. "From the church. You said it had no roof."

Ruth knows that she is right. "I'm so thick," she says. "I liked that wallpaper because it had a war memorial on it."

Evelyn laughs. "Now you can look at it and think of me instead," she says.

They finish their drinks and place the glasses on the floor by the bed, then shift down the mattress and turn onto their sides so that they are facing each other.

"Tell me what else is in the room," says Evelyn.

"There's a wardrobe. One of the doors squeaks, so I only ever open the other door, because I don't like the sound. There's a dressing table underneath the window."

"What's on it?"

"A small wooden tray that was my father's. He used to put his change into it at the end of every day. Now I put his watch in it before I go to sleep. Also, sometimes buttons that fall off my cardy and that I mean to sew back on."

"You're probably good at sewing because of your fly-tying," says Evelyn.

"Well, I never feel like it, so that tray is full of buttons, and no cardigan of mine has a full set."

"What else is on the dressing table?"

"A mirror. A hairbrush. Several tubes of lipstick."

"Lipstick. Very posh."

"For special occasions." Ruth squeezes Evelyn's hand back. "If I'd known you were on your way here."

"You'd have put some on?"

"I would."

Ruth traces her fingers across Evelyn's palm, feeling the smooth, raised welts, like thick worms, from where the fishing lure had once cut through Evelyn's skin.

"That's on my dressing table," says Evelyn. "In my jewellery box. The Highlander you tied for me."

"When you're dead, Ava will find it and think you liked to go fishing. Or that you once caught a really big salmon on that hook."

"Or someone will recognize your handiwork and the fly will be sold for hundreds of pounds."

"Ava can go on a holiday."

"Both of them can go." Evelyn moves Ruth's hand and places it on her stomach. "I'm pregnant again. Dan wants a son. Someone he can pass the farm on to."

There is a tightness to Evelyn's belly and a slight rounding. Ruth pulls back the flaps of the dressing gown and puts her hand on Evelyn's skin. Her hand is shaking. She hopes that Evelyn doesn't notice.

"How big is it now?" she asks.

"Perhaps the size of a chick or duckling. If it's a boy, Dan will probably want to name him after his father, Terence. If it's a girl"—Evelyn puts a hand up to Ruth's face and runs a finger along her lips—"I'm going to name her after you."

Even though Ruth is nervous, she is not surprised that Evelyn is here. She has imagined this moment countless times over the years, and the easy way they are talking with each other suggests that Evelyn has also imagined this. So, it is not a shock that they are together in Ruth's narrow single bed. This moment has already happened in both of their minds, and now it is simply a matter of their bodies catching up.

Ruth shifts her body closer to Evelyn's. They kiss, Ruth's hand still on Evelyn's belly. They kiss and press their bodies together. The rain continues. Socks comes into the bedroom and drops with a groan to the floor beside the bed. Ruth can feel the muscles across Evelyn's back, the sharp wings of her shoulder blades. The smell on her skin is hay and rain, the faint musk of lavender near Evelyn's collarbone.

Ruth means to stay awake all night, but she falls asleep with her arms around Evelyn, and wakes to Evelyn kneeling beside the bed, fully dressed, the room slowly filling with light.

"Ruth, I have to get home for the milking. Can you drive me?"

They hold hands in the car, when Ruth isn't shifting gears. At the farmhouse, Evelyn gets out of the car and then comes round to Ruth's side, knocks on the glass to make her roll down the window.

"I go to the village on Thursday afternoons," she says. "Dan drops me off and I take the bus back. I'm there between two and four."

"Tomorrow?"

"Yes. They should be home tonight, so I'll be there tomorrow."

But two fishermen up from Edinburgh drop by Ruth's on Thursday afternoon and she can't get away to go to the village. The next Thursday, Socks cuts his paw on a piece of wire fence and Ruth has to wait for the vet to come out to her cottage to sew it up. So, it is two weeks before she is able to, finally, meet up with Evelyn in Brora. She finds her at the post office with Ava in tow. They duck behind the display of envelopes and exercise books.

"Meet me at the war memorial after you're done here," says Evelyn.

"I'm so sorry," says Ruth. "There were these toffs the first week and then the vet last week."

Evelyn grabs hold of Ruth's coat sleeve and gives it a little shake. "I never doubted you," she says.

At the war memorial, they sit on the stone wall

to the side of the memorial tower. Evelyn gives Ava a packet of sweets, and the little girl cheerfully picks through them, choosing each one carefully and with great deliberation.

"Dan's moving us," says Evelyn. "His mother's going to give us her house and the farm. He's been wanting to switch from dairy to sheep for ages. His parents' farm does better than ours."

"When?"

"As soon as he can sell up here." Evelyn closes her hand over Ruth's. It's shaking. Ruth can't speak for fear she'll burst into tears.

"Barley sugar?" asks Ava, holding out the paper bag of sweets to her mother and her mother's friend. "You could have two each. They're my least favourite."

Silver Doctor

THEY ARRIVE BY TAXI FROM INVERNESS, AN extravagance that strikes Ruth as wasteful and a tad objectionable. There are two of them, a ginger and a dark-haired man. The ginger has a camera around his neck and fidgets with it constantly, even when he isn't lifting it to his eyes to take a photograph.

Ruth makes them tea and lays out some shortbread and chocolate fingers, but the men aren't content to sit in her parlour. They roam through the house, touching her pictures and books, peering into the framed portrait of her mother and father on their wedding day. She loads the tea onto a tray and moves them out to her work shed instead.

"So, this is where the magic happens," says the ginger when she opens the door and they step into the shed.

"It's not magic," says Ruth. "It's bloody hard work." She puts the tea tray down on the bench with the pile of orders on it. "And I'm always behind," she says, but they don't take the hint and hurry along. They poke through her cubbies of skins and feathers, touch her collection of bobbins and the packets of hooks on her work surface.

They photograph her sitting on her stool, tying a fly, her dog, Patch, sitting on the floor beside her, his head to one side, watching her work. Ruth thinks that he does this because he is intrigued by the feathers. No other dog of hers has chosen to observe her while she ties flies, but Patch considers her workday his own and accompanies her back and forth from the cottage to the shed, as though there is nothing else, even walking in the hills, that he would rather be doing.

"What is that you're making?" asks the dark-haired man, who, Ruth suddenly remembers, is called Damian.

"A Jock Scott. Classic salmon fly."

"But what is a Jock Scott?" says Damian. "It's not a thing."

"It was once a person," says Ruth.

"Yes, but how will the readers relate to it?" Damian puts his hand up to his head and taps his forehead. "Do you have something that's more descriptive?"

"Descriptive how?" Ruth hates to be interrupted in the middle of tying. She'll now have to start the Jock Scott from the beginning. She is wishing that she never agreed to this interview. Really, the last thing she needs is for hundreds of salmon fishers to read it and beat a path to her door. She's so far behind on her orders that she'll be tying flies long after she's died.

"Like a colour," says Damian. "Like, a totally green fly."

"There is no Green Fly," says Ruth. *I'm not tying you a Blue Charm*, she thinks to herself. "There's a Silver Doctor. Will that do?"

"Yes. Perfect." Damian takes a chocolate finger and then sets it back down on the plate. "It does have a lot of silver in it, doesn't it?"

Ruth holds up a bit of tinsel. "The body is wrapped in this," she says, "so it will be visible in a colour photograph."

The men pace the work shed, looking for the best angle for the photographs. The ginger, whose name is Norman, takes some shots close up and then goes outside to photograph Ruth through the shed window. It is disconcerting to look up and see the camera and the face where she usually sees the calm, flat stretch of North Sea, so Ruth keeps her head bowed, concentrating on her work.

While she is being photographed, Damian asks Ruth questions: how she got started in this business, how many clients she has, what does she think of the new trend to use animal fur in salmon flies, rather than feathers.

"Many of the feathers you use for certain flies are endangered or protected," he says. "Why not use squirrel tail instead?"

"I'm only interested in the classic salmon flies," says Ruth. "That's what I know how to do."

"So, no substitutes?"

"If a bird whose feathers I use becomes protected, I simply stop tying that fly."

After the questions and the photographs, the men go out into the garden to smoke. They can't call a taxi from Ruth's cottage because she has no telephone, so she will have to drive them into the village to make a call from the lobby of the hotel. Luckily, it is Thursday, which is her day for going into Brora anyway.

The journalists come back into the shed for one last look around, to make sure they haven't missed something terrifically photogenic.

"It's strange to see oaks in Scotland," says Norman, nodding to the window and the line of young oak trees at the bottom of Ruth's garden.

She drives them into the village, leaving Patch at home. After dropping them at the hotel, Ruth fills her water jugs and then goes to the post office to send off some orders. She waits in line behind Mrs. McGrath, who is one of the old ladies that Ruth plays whist with most Saturday nights. Her knees have been bothering her lately, so she doesn't dance as often as she used to, and now plays cards to try to keep up her social life.

"Lovely day," says Mrs. McGrath.

It is another grey day in a series of grey days, but periodically, the sun bursts through the clouds, so Ruth agrees that it is better than it has been.

"I thought you'd be interested to know that I was down in Inverness last week," says Mrs. McGrath, "and I saw Mrs. Munro outside the chemist's with her two children."

"Who?"

"Evelyn. She is married to Dan. They lived in the farm just down the road from you."

Ruth can feel herself flush.

"Oh, yes, I remember her," she says, trying to sound casual. "Was she well?"

"Very well. Nice-looking daughters. Tall and willowy like their mother." It is Mrs. McGrath's turn at the window, but Ruth can't let her go without another question.

"Do you remember the name of her second daughter?" she asks. "They moved before she had the baby."

"Eileen," says Mrs. McGrath, turning away from Ruth and pushing her pension book across the counter to the clerk.

Ruth posts her packages, goes to the butcher to get some chops for her tea. On her way back to her car, she sits for a moment on the wall beside the war memorial, watching the traffic swish past.

She has the door of her car open when she hears a voice calling her name. It's Mrs. McGrath, hurrying over the pavement towards her.

"I was wrong," she says. "You'd think I would have remembered, on account of you."

"Remember what?" says Ruth.

"Evelyn's youngest isn't called Eileen. Her name is Ruth Eileen."

Ruth drives home, lugs the jugs of water inside from her car boot, stows her groceries in the larder. Then she takes Patch out. They walk farther than usual today, up into the hills that rise behind her cottage. She climbs and climbs, out of breath and panting, her feet slipping on the mud and stones. When she is high enough, she turns towards the sea and looks down the coast road until she can spy Evelyn's old house. The Munros' farm was bought by two brothers from Helmsdale, bachelors who barely come down into the village. She can't tell, from this height and distance, what they have changed about the place and what they have left alone. She can see the house, the dark shape of the barn, the square of the farmyard and the rust-coloured fields tilting into the horizon beyond that.

Back home, Ruth feeds the dog, makes some tea, carries it across to her work shed. She ties flies well into the evening. These days, she has so many orders that she has broken her own rule of only tying during the daylight hours, and she works past civil twilight, right into the darkness, two paraffin lamps burning on the table either side of her, as though she is a ship at sea.

The magazine article appears, and for a few weeks, a different fisherman shows up at her door every day, inspired by the interview to pay Ruth a visit and order some salmon flies from her. It is as she feared and just makes her busier than ever. She now ties right up until midnight, whether it is summer or winter, using the paraffin lamps to light up her workspace during the night. She no longer listens to programs on the wireless or does any of her DIY jobs. The wallpaper she has up in her cottage will remain there until the end of her days. She plays whist most Saturday nights, and sometimes on Sundays she will take one or two of the elderly people in the village out for a drive in the country, but she no longer goes for lengthy drives herself, and never goes to Glen of the Fairies anymore. For a long time after her disastrous date with Graham, it was her destination of choice for a Sunday outing. She liked the landscape there, the stark beauty of the hills and becks, the fact that it was far enough away from home that she never ran into anyone she knew.

Ruth works so much that everything else is just an interruption, and she feels guilty for any time away from her fly-tying desk. There are fewer and fewer fly dressers who are adept with the classic salmon fly patterns, and Ruth would like to pass on her knowledge to an apprentice, but the young men who have shown up at her door wanting to be taught prove to be not very good at it, or too slow, or they make her too slow. In teaching, Ruth realizes that certain things can't be taught, and that a natural ability exists or it doesn't, and if it does exist, it can be encouraged and fostered, but if it doesn't exist, it can't be learned.

There is no heir to take over Ruth's business, so she just keeps going. In her fifties, she is working harder than she did in her thirties, but her body isn't as forgiving. She has gained weight from sitting still for so long at the vise, and her knees hurt. Her neck aches from the way she bends over while working, and her eyes have started to fail. She now has to use a magnifying glass to tie most flies and has purchased one that clips to her vise so that she can still use both hands in her work.

She now eats supper late in the evening, gobbling it down before collapsing into bed. When she wakes again six hours later, she can't remember falling asleep. The sleep is so deep and lasting, it feels like death.

Patch dies of old age and is replaced by Percy, a scruffy little brown terrier. Ruth can't manage the big sheepdogs anymore, especially as puppies, but she is unsure whether she will take to a smaller dog. Percy, however, has a large personality and proves to be a worthy successor to Patch. He also likes to watch Ruth work, sitting beside her on a chair with a cushion on it, pawing at her to remind her to take him for a walk or feed him his supper or go to bed. Percy is a stickler for the rules, and if Ruth works later than he thinks she should, he will bark at her sharply until she blows out the lamps, and they cross the lawn to the cottage.

All through the years, Ruth has held out hope that Evelyn will just show up again one day, but she never does. When Ruth goes into her bedroom at night, she runs her hand along the wallpaper before getting under the covers, looking at the memorial steeple perched on its patch of grass, entwined with roses.

The oak trees grow into a screen and protect the garden from the winds that tumble in off the North Sea. Each autumn, the trees release a rain of acorns onto the lawn, and Ruth collects a bowlful and puts them on the little table in her parlour, next to the wireless.

Eliza writes from her life in southern England to say that their mother has died in her sleep, so Ruth travels down by train, leaving Percy with friends. She sits in Eliza's front room and makes small talk with her sisters, whom she hasn't seen in years. They have never come back to Brora, and Ruth has seldom had the time to travel south to see them. Their grown children tower over her at the funeral, and she muddles their names. There is cake, little sandwiches on white bread without the crusts, and large pots of tea at the reception. Many people come to pay their respects, none of them known to Ruth. She stands at the graveside, watching the coffin as it is lowered into its sleeve of wet earth and she feels nothing. On the train northward, she watches the buildings fade out to the Scottish heath and hills and is relieved to be back home again.

Popham

AT FIRST, HE SENDS HIS ORDERS IN BY POST, on the thick Royal stationery with the heavy red seal. When the flies are ready, he dispatches a car and driver out to Ruth's cottage to pick them up, or she drops them round at the hotel where he stays when he is in Brora to fish. But after a year or two of this arrangement, he begins to come out himself to the cottage, leaving his car and driver to wait in the lane while he visits with Ruth and collects his salmon flies. The Prince likes to sit on the rickety wooden chair in her work shed and talk with Ruth about the different flies she makes. He is a connoisseur of the classic salmon fly, a purist like Ruth, and he appreciates the care and attention to detail that she takes with each one of her creations.

"You are a true artist," he says. "I would like to bring you to the world's attention."

"I have too much attention already," says Ruth. "I won't be wanting any more, thank you."

But the Prince arranges for her to be awarded a medal from the Queen, and they have the presentation at his hunting lodge when he is up for the summer. After the ceremony, Ruth has tea with the Prince and his entourage at the lodge and then leaves for home in her car, stopping briefly at the cemetery where her father is buried.

"Daddy," she says, standing at his grave, holding the medal above his tombstone, "look what they gave me today for dressing flies." She knows he would be proud of her, his little Ruthie, now a stout, grey-haired woman in her middle fifties.

The Prince likes the Popham.

"It's the most elegant of flies, don't you agree?" he says.

It is a complicated fly, one of the hardest to tie, with a multitude of components. Ruth likes it because it is so hard to make, which she thinks is a tad snobbish on her part, but she also feels she has earned that right.

"It is my favourite as well," she says.

"Will you show me how it's done?" The Prince

likes to stand beside her while she works, much like her dogs have done, watching as she winds thread onto a hook, deftly attaches feather and hackle.

Ruth clamps a hook in her vise, positions the magnifier above it as she reaches for a bobbin.

"My eyes aren't what they used to be," she says to the Prince.

"It's fiddly work, isn't it," he says. "And you are working the way the classic fly dressers did." What he means is that Ruth has no electricity. The Prince has romanticized Ruth's spartan living conditions to support his view of her as a true master of the salmon fly.

Summer turns to autumn and the days shorten correspondingly. Ruth is often busiest in the spring and fall. In the spring, the fishermen and the salmon are both excited to be back on the rivers. In the fall, the fishermen are desperate to get as much time in on the rivers as they can before winter puts a temporary stop to their passion.

The Prince returns south and Ruth redoubles her efforts to tie as many flies as she can during the course of a day. It feels harder now to fit in everything else, to make the time each week to go to the village and pick up water, post her packages of flies off to the customers, some of whom have been waiting years to receive their original "Ruth Thomas." She is always rushing and she always feels constantly exhausted.

But there is an unexpected gift to this autumn, a return to her life of someone from her past.

He arrives at her cottage on a Saturday morning, rapping sharply on her shed window and startling her while she is working. When she opens the door, he grins at her from the threshold, extending his arms out for an embrace.

"You look just the same," he says when Ruth steps forward into his arms.

"You also," she says. But they have both aged, and she knows that he notices it as well. He is still dashing in his way, but Captain Asher is balding and barrel-chested now. When he walks across the lawn, there is a stiffness and caution to his gait.

"Fused discs," he says as they stroll down to the row of oak trees at the bottom of the garden. "Some days, it's even hard to tie my shoes." He reaches out and touches the trunk of the nearest oak. "Bloody marvellous," he says. "Your little bit of Surrey in Scotland."

"It's really your little bit of Surrey," says Ruth.

He takes her for lunch at the hotel, and for once, Ruth puts aside her work and doesn't feel guilty about it. They huddle together in the snug, eating fish and chips. Captain Asher has a pint and Ruth has a half shandy.

"Special occasion," she says, raising her glass.

"I knew you'd still be here," says John (and after all this time, Ruth finally feels comfortable calling him by his given name). "Sarah said I was mad to come and look for you in the last place I'd seen you, but I knew you would stay put, that you would be here for life." He takes a long swallow of his beer. "Because why would you leave? The biggest reasons to move are love and work. Your work is here, and you're not the marrying kind."

"That makes me sound so dull," says Ruth. "I could have married. There was someone who once tried to woo me."

"But you weren't interested, were you?" John puts down his glass. "Because you are an independent spirit and you would have to give up that independence to marry and have children."

"Well, that's not really it," says Ruth. "I just didn't fancy him. Even though I tried to." The shandy is going to her head. She has Evelyn's name on the tip of her tongue, wants to tell Captain Asher that there was someone she did care for, but she is not sure how he will respond.

"Did you really come all this way to see me?" she asks instead.

"And to go fishing. I retired from work this year and this trip is my reward to myself for all those years of mindless toil."

"Are you going out on the Brora?"

"Yes. I've booked a room here at the hotel for the better part of a week. I mean to be out on the river every day."

"You'll need a gillie. I could spend afternoons guiding you, if you wanted."

"I would love that, but aren't you overworked enough already?"

"I will never be caught up with my orders," says Ruth. "I'm reconciled to that now. For a long time, I thought that I could catch up, but I don't think it's actually possible." She finishes her shandy, sets the glass back down on the table next to John's empty pint glass. "So, hang the orders. I would like to go and visit with the Brora again, and to do it with you."

For the week that John Asher is in Scotland, they fall into an easy routine together. Ruth spends the morning working in her shed, and after a hurried lunch, sometimes eaten in the car while she is driving, she goes down to the hotel to pick him up.

They visit a different pool on the Lower Brora every day. Ruth sits on the bank and watches John sling his line into the water. She has seen her fair share of casters and he is not half bad at it.

"You're in the top sector," she says.

"Who's the best?"

"Believe it or not, HRH."

"Well, he has all the time in the world for fishing, doesn't he?" John wades farther into the river.

"It's not that. There are people who spend more time on the rivers than he does. I don't even think that he fishes that often. It's more that he's very precise when he does." That is what the Prince and Ruth have in common, and what they recognize and admire in each other, a love of, and a belief in, perfection.

A duck has the temerity to cross into Percy's territory and he races along the riverbank towards it, barking his warning.

"Noisier than Sergeant Socks," says John.

"Noisier than any of my dogs." Ruth watches as Percy trots back towards them, his tail held high. "But also a good deal more spirited, so I forgive him his outbursts."

In the evenings, Ruth dines with John at the hotel. It is a tremendous relief not to be boiling eggs or heating up a tin of beans, slapping a chop in the pan. She orders from a menu, has a shandy with every supper, and John Asher pays for the lot.

"I don't know who is having the better holiday," she says. "You or me."

When she goes home at the end of every day that week, she sleeps soundly and has peaceful dreams. No one chases her through the hills, but rather, she is climbing a hill with Evelyn by her side, and when they get to the top, they look out on the most beautiful view, a cascade of hills with the shiny blue crinkle of ocean in the distance.

On their last day together, Ruth takes John to the Madman pool. The water is lower than usual because of the unusually dry summer, but the pool is one of the larger ones on the Brora and is a good spot for salmon.

John wades out into the water, and because it is their last day on the river, Ruth takes off her shoes and stockings and wades out with him into the current. Percy, who objects to this and can't follow Ruth into the water because he doesn't really like to get wet, runs up and down the bank instead, voicing his severe displeasure.

The water is cold, noses up against Ruth's legs as she moves unsteadily out into the current.

"When we first came to Scotland," she says, "I walked down to this river with my father and we waded out into it like we're doing now. All the salmon moving through it made it feel alive, like an animal itself. It was the first thing I loved about this place."

John flicks his line upriver, lets it drift back down.

"If we're lucky," he says, "we get to circle back in life."

"And if we live long enough," says Ruth.

At their last dinner together, John Asher orders a half bottle of champagne and they make a toast to old times and absent friends.

"Don't let another thirty years go by before you come back again," says Ruth.

"I won't. And I'll bring Sarah with me next time. You would like each other."

"I would love that. And to meet your children."

After dinner, they stand out in front of the hotel, watching the stars for a moment before Ruth gets into her car and drives home. It is a clear night and the heavens are full.

"It might sound strange because the war was a terrible time for most people," Ruth says, "but I was very happy then."

"Yes. Perhaps it was the not knowing what was going to happen next. We were living as I imagine animals mostly exist, which I think is probably a good way to live. On nerves and feelings." John opens the car door for her. "I will miss you, Private Thomas."

"And I will miss you, Captain Asher."

They embrace, holding onto each other for as long as seems reasonable, and then breaking apart abruptly. Ruth gets into her car and slips it into gear. John stands out front of the hotel, a hand raised in farewell. Ruth looks in her rear-view mirror and sees him standing perfectly still in the halo of light spilling from the hotel sign.

She drives the coast road past the turnoff for her cottage, right up to the headland, past the spots where the old coastwatching huts used to stand. They are long gone now, knocked down years ago after first being defaced with graffiti. One was even set on fire.

At the farthest point up the coast road, at the top of the headland, Ruth pulls the car over to the shoulder and shuts off the engine and the lamps. She gets out and leans against the bonnet, looking out across the dark blank of the North Sea, the wind twisting around her body. At first there is nothing, but if she looks hard enough, she can see that far out, there is a single light, faint and distant, moving slowly farther north.

Jock Scott

At first, Ruth can make compensations for her failing eyesight. She stops driving at night. She orders a more powerful magnifier for her fly dressing. Her house is so familiar to her that she can find her way through it instinctively. But increasingly, her worsening vision becomes a problem. She notices at her whist games that she can no longer see sideways out of her eyes, that the card player sitting on her left is effectively no longer there.

"You should have your eyes checked," says the Prince when he notices her squinting through her new magnifier. "Get fitted for some spectacles. I know a good man in London. I could make the arrangements for you."

"There's no one to look after Percy if I go all the way to London."

"I'll tell you what," says the Prince. "I will have my driver take you to the appointment and you can bring the dog with you and leave him in the car while you're at the doctor's."

So, Ruth is driven all the way to Harley Street in London with Percy curled up on the seat beside her, as though they were royalty themselves.

The doctor makes her look through various lenses at faraway letters on a white board. Then he shines a light at the side of her eyes, moving it in an arc towards the front and asking when she can see it and when it disappears.

The room is dark and the chair Ruth has been given to sit in is comfortable. It tilts a little backwards in a most relaxing way. She has to struggle not to fall asleep, even with the helmeted contraption with lenses that the doctor has placed over her head.

At the end of the appointment, the doctor switches on the overhead lights and moves his chair close to hers.

"I'm afraid it's bad news," he says. "You have macular degeneration."

"What does that mean?"

"You're going blind. It's irreversible. Your sight will gradually disappear until you can no longer see at all."

Ruth isn't one for crying, but she cries on the way home in the car, hugging Percy to her chest. When the Prince comes to see her the next day, she tells him the prognosis and is touched that he seems nearly as upset as she is.

"That's terrible," he says. "There must be an operation that you can have. I will do some investigating."

But even with his Royal concern and probing, there is nothing that can be done for Ruth's sight. She tries to continue on as before, but she knows now that her fly-dressing days are coming to a close.

What she would like is for there to be someone she could pass her business on to, but there are no likely candidates in the immediate area. She contacts her sister Marjory's son, Jack, and manages to entice him north for a weekend.

He lumbers out of the train station, clutching his valise, which he balances carefully across his knees in the car, waving away Ruth's attempt to put it in the boot.

"Do you have the Crown jewels in there?" she says, trying to make a joke, but he just glowers at her.

At the cottage, Ruth throws open the gate, leading Jack over the lawn to her shed.

"Is this it?" he asks, peering through the doorway.

For the first day, her nephew sits uncomfortably beside her at her work table, sweat from his forehead dripping onto the little twist of blue feather he is trying to tie onto the hook. He is clumsy and his fingers are too fat for precision. The feather clumps together and the fly looks like it's already underwater.

That evening, Jack eats two helpings of sausages and mash and then bolts down the hallway to his bedroom. Ruth goes back out to her shed and ties flies by lamplight until she is too tired to continue. When she passes Jack's bedroom on the way to her own, she can hear him talking animatedly to himself.

The second day is no better, and by afternoon, Ruth has lost patience with the whole enterprise and tells her nephew to go for a walk so that she can get some orders filled.

He disappears and doesn't come back, but when Ruth goes in to make the tea, she can hear him laughing from behind his closed bedroom door. She watches him intently while they eat together, but he seems perfectly normal, albeit a little surly.

Immediately after he's eaten, he goes back into the spare bedroom. Ruth stands outside with her ear pressed to the door and can hear him talking to himself again. She opens the door and walks into the room.

Jack is sitting on the floor. He has headphones clamped over his ears and his valise is open beside him. It is not a valise at all, but a radio. There is a microphone on a stand in front of the valise and Jack is crouched over that, speaking into it. He doesn't hear the door open and Ruth has to tap him on the shoulder to get his attention.

"What are you doing?" she says.

Jack pulls the headphones off.

"Talking to PD681," he says.

"Who is PD681?"

"A man from Holland."

"Are you a spy?"

Jack laughs. "I wish I was," he says. "No, it's just my hobby." He points to the inside of the valise, where Ruth can see a long list of numbers written neatly across the lid. "I talk to people all over the world."

Ruth sits down on the edge of the bed. "Let's have a listen then," she says.

They stay up late, calling the other side of the world where it's already morning, the static through the headphones reminding Ruth of the distance their voices are travelling to reach each other.

At the station the next morning, Ruth hugs her nephew and means it.

"I'm sorry it didn't work out," she says.

"Yes," he says, hugging her back. "I thought tying flies might be the sort of thing I could do while I talked on the radio, but it's not like that at all."

There are fewer hours in the day that Ruth can dress flies now. She needs to save what remaining sight she has for the other tasks of her life, for cooking meals and managing her little household. She still drives her car, because she doesn't quite know how she'd get by without it, but she only drives in full daylight and is more cautious than she used to be.

She practises tying flies with her eyes closed and can do it just fine, but it will be a slow production if that is how she has to manage when she is completely blind. And how will she read the orders that come through the post?

She finds a care home nearby in Golspie that will take her when the time comes, and then she waits for Percy to die, because she can't bear to give him up. When he finally does get cancer, at the age of twelve, and has to be put down, she weeps over his little body at the vet's, and then drives back home and immediately packs her bags. By this time, she has already given much of her fly-tying equipment to a friend who dresses flies in Helmsdale, including her vise, bobbins and tinsel, and bird skins. The rest of the materials and her table full of orders, she just leaves in the shed, turning the key in the lock and stepping away from the building, and the life, in which she has lived wholly and intimately for the past fifty-five years.

Ruth drives her car to a friend's house, and her friend, in turn, drives her to the care home in Golspie. The car is to be given to another friend. Her cottage has just been abandoned. Lady Drummond is long dead, but the cottage still belongs to the estate and will be absorbed back into it.

Ruth is given a south-facing room in the care home and she appreciates the light that fills the window most of the day, but her eyesight is almost gone at this point and so it is difficult to navigate the passageways of the home. She never knows where she is and sometimes forgets that she isn't in her cottage anymore, feeling along the hallways for the right texture of wallpaper to tell her what room she's entered. Sometimes, she is so lost that she has to stop and cry out until someone comes along to rescue her.

Friends still visit. She is loved and not abandoned by those who know her. But she cannot help the fishermen anymore and this upsets Ruth. She cannot help anyone. In the fullness of her life, she was always ready to drive a friend to a medical appointment, take a lonely widow on a day out to the countryside, or help another friend to set mousetraps. Now she cannot even help herself. She cannot even find her way around the place where she now lives. Her surroundings are all suddenly mysterious and frightening.

She misses Percy. There was such personality packed into his little body and she feels empty without his fierce company. She wishes she'd given him all the nuggets of cheese and scraps of toast he had begged for.

One day, Ruth is sitting by the window, enjoying the feeling of the sun on her face, when the door to her room clicks softly open. She hears the pad of feet over carpet.

"Hello. Who's there?"

There's the sound of a chair being dragged closer to the window, and then a hand lightly touches her shoulder.

"It's me, Ruth."

The voice is the same, even after all these years. Ruth reaches over and finds Evelyn's hand.

"How did you know where to find me?"

"I went to the cottage. Someone has put a notice on the door saying you are here in Golspie. For the fishermen, I suppose. To stop them from coming."

"They show up anyway from time to time," says Ruth. "I still tie the odd fly. Fishermen, it turns out, are as hard to stop in their habits as salmon." She pauses. "I'm blind now."

Evelyn squeezes her hand. "I know that," she says.

"If this is a dream, it's a very nice one," says Ruth.

"It's not a dream."

"Am I dying?"

"I think you might be," Evelyn says.

"I waited for so long."

"I know."

"And you're only here now?"

"I couldn't come before. I had to wait for Dan to die." Evelyn leans closer to Ruth. "It was impossible otherwise. It was so hard for me to come to you at all, but you have to understand that I did whenever I could."

Ruth puts her hand up and touches Evelyn's face. The skin is soft with age.

"Do you remember the castle?" Ruth says.

"Of course."

"I think that was when I was the most happy."

"I was going to say the same."

They sit quietly. Ruth can feel the warmth of the sun through the window. In her mind, she is tying flies, marrying feather to hook, seeing herself sitting at her stool in the little shed overlooking the North Sea, everything she needs exactly to hand. And now, walking down the castle steps with Evelyn, the lawn dark as water before them. The drift of rosemary from the terrace.

And when death comes then for Ruth, it comes as one of her salmon flies, arcing through the darkness towards her. She shudders her body up to meet it, opens her mouth. Swallows it whole.

The fish move together up the river, their bodies churning through the water.

"Where are they going?" asks Ruth.

"To spawn and die," says Arthur.

"But I don't want them to die."

Arthur bends down so that his head is level with his daughter's.

"Look at them, Ruthie," he says. "They are so full of themselves. They are doing exactly what they want to be doing. No one is their master."

His face is so close to Ruth's that she can feel his words on her skin when he speaks them. He gives her shoulders a squeeze.

"They are so full of life," he says, "that they won't even notice they have died."

Acknowledgements

I would like to thank my agent, Clare Alexander, and my editor, Jennifer Lambert, for their care and wisdom during the writing of this book.

Thanks also to Mary Louise Adams, Tama Baldwin, Nancy Jo Cullen, Eleanor MacDonald, Kirsteen MacLeod, Marco Reiter, Ray and Lori Vos, Jane Warren and Noelle Zitzer.

Special thanks to the esteemed and beloved members of the BDL.

My gratitude to Anne Hardcastle, for leading me to Megan Boyd.

Thanks to the National Water Centre in Saint John, New Brunswick, for a residency in 2016, during which some of this book was written.

Further information on Megan Boyd can be found in the book *Megan Boyd: The Story of a*

Salmon Flydresser (2016), by Derek Mills and Jimmy Younger, and the documentary film *Kiss the Water* (2013), directed by Eric Steel.

The book's epigraph is from the poetry collection *Ariel* (1965), by Sylvia Plath, and is used with permission from Faber & Faber Ltd. The poems quoted in the chapter "Blue Charm" are "Afton Water" (Sweet Afton) and "A Red, Red Rose," both by Robert Burns. The poem quoted in the chapter "Thunder and Lightning" is "Dover Beach" by Matthew Arnold.